CHRISTMAS
at
HARMONY HILL

CHRISTMAS
at
HARMONY HILL

A SHAKER STORY

ANN H. GABHART

R
Revell
a division of Baker Publishing Group
Grand Rapids, Michigan

Published by Revell
a division of Baker Publishing Group
P.O. Box 6287, Grand Rapids, MI 49516-6287
www.revellbooks.com

Printed in the United States of America

Library of Congress Cataloging-in-Publication Data
Gabhart, Ann H., 1947–
    Christmas at Harmony Hill : a Shaker story / Ann H. Gabhart.
      pages cm
    ISBN 978-0-8007-1982-1 (cloth)
      1. Pregnant women—Fiction. 2. Pregnant women—Family relationships—Fiction. 3. Abandoned children—Fiction. 4. Shakers—Fiction. I. Title.
    PS3607.A23C47 2013
    813'.6—dc23   2013017656

Scripture used in this book, whether quoted or paraphrased by the characters, is taken from the King James Version of the Bible.

13 14 15 16 17 18 19   7 6 5 4 3 2 1

In memory of my aunt,
Lorin Bond Houchin,
who always made Christmas special

1

*H*eather Worth sat propped against her washboard, listening to her husband's light snores. Gideon could sleep anywhere. Out on the hard ground of a battlefield. In a tent with her on washer row. A man needed his rest to fight the war and push the Johnny Rebs back south. She needed the same. It was no easy task being the army company's laundress, but she wouldn't be washing any uniforms on the morrow. She could sit and wait for the dawn to light up the face she loved.

She clasped her hands in her lap to keep from reaching out to brush the red hair back from his forehead. Her fingers itched to trace across his cheeks and memorize the exact position of his every freckle. She wished him awake, but he slept on. She'd known him to sleep sound as a baby with the Confederates so near they could hear them singing around their campfires.

None of the enemy was that close now, but come daylight, the army was heading toward Tennessee to chase after them. It had to be done, the officers said. Heather had heard them talking. None of them paid any mind to the washerwoman, as if they didn't think she could hear over the slosh of washtubs. But she heard plenty and the plenty she heard saddened her heart. They were saying they might have to root out and shoot every last one of the Rebels before they could get this war over. Her brother was one of those Rebels. Because Simon wasn't even a whole year younger than she was, they'd grown up almost like twins. The day after Simon turned eighteen, he'd gone south to join the Confederate Army. A month later she left home to marry Gideon.

That had been two long years ago. Two years of washing uniforms for the privilege of following the army. At least it was honorable work, and when no battle was raging, Gideon slept beside her on washer row. Now here in November 1864, the word was General Sherman had taken Atlanta and was headed to the sea, but even that wasn't making the Confederates surrender.

So Gideon's division was headed to Nashville. Off to fight Hood. War was like wildfire. The army stomped it down in one place and the flames scooted out and started up in another place. Heather hated war. Everything about it. The blood on the uniforms she washed. The smell inside the surgeons' tents after the wounds went putrid. The dying men who begged her to write one last letter to their families. She hated it all. Even the times between battles. Living in the open. No house to call her own. Nothing but guns and dirty uniforms. But she loved Gideon. So much that she'd become a camp follower against her father's wishes.

She put a hand up in the dark to block out the memory of his hurtful words. She didn't want to think about her father. This night was Gideon's. But then a dark sliver of her father's anger sliced through her. How could Gideon keep on snoring when this might be the last night they would ever be together?

He had told her she shouldn't think that way. "Two years I've been out here fighting the Rebs without catching a bullet," he said the night before, right after he held her tight and told her she had to go home. That she couldn't follow the army to Tennessee.

She had hidden the swell of the baby growing inside her for months. Even after Gideon knew, they'd delayed her leaving, although he worried about her wrestling the wash pots. She was strong. She could manage. Had managed. Her hands went to her abdomen and caressed the baby tumbling about inside her as though trying to push through her skin to know this last moment with his father.

She almost wished he could, but by her reckoning, it was nearly two months too soon. If they hadn't gotten orders to march south, she might have talked Gideon into letting her stay. But he'd shuddered at the thought of his son being born on a battlefield.

To pull his mind away from the bad memories of those conflicts, she had smiled and said, "Son? What if I carry a girl with red hair like her father?"

No smile came to his face in answer to hers. "Even more I wouldn't want my daughter born in the midst of blood and killing." He leaned over to kiss her rounded stomach, then looked back at her face. "Go home."

Home. The word struck a chord in Heather's heart. She wanted to be home. She wanted her mother to help her bring her child into the world. Gideon was right. A battleground with death hovering over it was no place to birth an innocent babe.

So she said yes. Always before, she had said no, she wouldn't leave Gideon. But last night she agreed to go. She had no other answer. The tubs were getting too heavy for her with the weight of her unborn child dragging her down. So she'd retreat back to her Kentucky home. Her mother wouldn't let her father turn her away. Not when she saw Heather heavy with child.

Heather shifted against the washboard. Her back did ache. No matter what position she tried.

The black of the night softened to a gentle gray. Feet passed by on the other side of the tent wall. The soldier husband of Jenna, the other washerwoman. Jenna's washtubs clanged as she began packing up. Her two boys would be helping her. Heather thought to slip out of the tent to offer Jenna her own tubs and wooden stir paddles.

She moved to get up, but Gideon woke to pull her down beside him for one last embrace before the war ripped them apart. Gideon was right. She shouldn't complain. She'd had more of him than most wives whose husbands marched off to war. He ran his hand over the baby bulge under her skirt. She hadn't put on nightclothes the evening before. She slept in her dress more times than not. Not much privacy on washer row.

She lay silent in Gideon's arms as he whispered love words in her ear. That was what had made her fall in love with him. The way he talked. The way he laughed. How could she bear not seeing that smile for weeks, perhaps months? Maybe never again.

"I won't smile again until we're together once more," she whispered.

A frown crossed his face. "No, no, my Heather Lou. Don't let your smile get rusty. Keep it all practiced up so that it will come easy when you see me coming home to you and our sweet little babe." His eyes softened on her. "You are so beautiful. So very beautiful." His voice was husky.

She almost laughed then, thinking how far from beautiful she must look after living in an army camp for so long. Her hands were red and raw from the soap and scrubbing. Her face windburned. Her dark hair, twisted in a bun to keep it out of the way, was streaked by too many hours in the sun. Bonnets were a luxury in an army camp. A kerchief was all one could expect. Her dress was sturdy but plain and lacking the first hint of feminine frill.

"Only in your eyes," she said.

"My eyes are the ones that matter." He put his hand on her cheek and studied her face. "I'll carry this vision with me until the war is over."

"Will that ever happen?" It seemed to Heather as if the war had been going on forever.

"They're beat. They just don't know it yet. But they will soon, and when that happens, I'll be running home to you." He tapped her nose with his finger. "We'll have a little house and every night, every livelong night, we'll lie like this and talk about whether the hens are laying or if the corn's ready to pick."

"Will we be happy?"

"We'll be happy as two birds in a ripe blackberry patch, my Heather Lou."

One more embrace and then he was pulling on his boots, buttoning his shirt, slipping the braces up over his shoulders to hold up his trousers. Turning from her Gideon into a soldier. Tents had to be taken down. Everything carried on to the next fighting spot. Heather had done it all over and over. Fold this. Roll that. Make it fit on the wagon or leave it behind. Now she was what didn't fit. What was going to be left behind.

She watched the company form and march away. Gideon risked the ire of his captain by breaking rank for one last goodbye kiss. The other soldiers whistled and made catcalls, but Gideon wasn't bothered. That was the thing about Gideon. He was ready to dance to whatever tune the day might be playing. But he promised to always give her the first and last dance.

The baby twisted and kicked inside her as he turned to run back in line. The captain was yelling at him, but with no anger in his voice as he looked over toward Heather and winked. A good number of the men lifted a hand and waved as they passed. For months, she'd been scrubbing their clothes and paying mind to their talk of families back home.

Good men. She didn't want to think about any of them charging the enemy's artillery. She wished rock fences for them to hide behind. She'd seen too many wounded men. Too many bodies waiting burial. What if this time that fate befell Gideon? Fear squeezed her heart and a prayer rose unbidden within her.

Dear Father in heaven, protect my Gideon. Don't let him be too brave. Protect them all.

He was still looking back at her, so she kept her lips turned up in what would pass for a smile with the distance separating them. A distance that grew farther every second. She wanted to run along the road after him in order to see him one minute longer, but then he was turning with his face forward. Facing his future. She had no choice but to do the same.

When she could no longer even imagine seeing a glimpse of his hat, she picked up her valise and headed toward the town. It wasn't far, only a mile or two. She could get a train ticket to Kentucky, to home. She'd go as far as the train would take her and walk the rest of the way. Hadn't she walked miles and miles across Kentucky and Virginia as the two armies searched out each other to see who could do the most dying?

She put a hand on the swell of her stomach and a bit of Scripture came to her. *Be of good courage, and he shall strengthen your heart, all ye that hope in the Lord.*

She did hope in the Lord. She did. Pray God, so did Gideon.

2

*L*ooking back to catch a last glimpse of Heather, Gideon stumbled over his own feet and almost fell. The big man beside him grabbed hold of his arm to keep him upright and moving forward.

Gideon turned his face resolutely south as he got back into step. "You can turn loose of me now."

Jake White laughed and grasped Gideon's arm all the tighter. "I'm feared to turn you loose, lad. Afraid you'll be deserting the likes of us for your pretty washerwoman."

Jake had come over from Ireland a few years before. He'd joined up with the Union Army saying he'd seen Ireland fall apart with the hunger parting families and he wasn't wanting to see his new country rent asunder as well. Already into his thirties, he was years older than most of the soldiers, but he lacked family to tie him to home. He'd had a wife, but she'd been carried off by a fever.

"I feel like I'm deserting her." Gideon glanced over his shoulder, but there was nothing but more men marching along behind him. No girl in a dark blue dress chasing after him.

"Aye, that you are," Jake agreed pleasantly. "But a soldier marches where the generals order."

"She's carrying my child," Gideon said.

"Noticed as much the last time she laundered my uniform." Jake let go of Gideon's arm at last and looked straight ahead. His next words carried a weary sadness. "My Irene, she was in the family way when the fever took her."

"But you didn't desert her."

"Nay, I did not, but the enemy won nevertheless." He sighed before he shook himself like a dog after a dip in a pond. "But that has naught to do with your bonny lass. She's a strong one in spite of her winsome looks. Else she couldn't have followed the army these months. She'll be glad for the rest of going home to birth your little one."

"Her father was against her wedding me."

"What did you expect, lad? A skinny excuse for a man like you showing up to steal his daughter. You don't look like you'd last two rows hoeing corn."

"I never did take to hoeing," Gideon said with a laugh. "Of course, I never thought to take to soldiering either."

"But here you are."

"Here I am." Gideon peeked back over his shoulder in hopes she'd run along after the troops so he could feast his eyes on her yet one more time. But that wasn't Heather's way. That was more the sort of thing he would do. Think nothing of the consequences but follow the whim of the moment. That's why he'd risked the ire of the captain and broken rank to give her one last kiss. A kiss she'd remember the more for it being unexpected.

He'd think on that kiss and the look on her face and keep back the weariness of the march. Sometimes it was better to think about what had been rather than what was ahead. And what had been were many sweet nights with his Heather Lou.

3

The train jerked and bounced across country. Heather had been on trains before when the army, including her and her wash pots, moved by rail, but never for so many miles. She felt swallowed up by the belching iron monster with its windows blackened by smoke and people elbowing their way up the aisles on and off at every stop.

One seat companion urged her to lean back and sleep away the journey, but he had a shady look and eyes that rested too often on her valise. She thought it best to keep her own eyes open. A woman alone needed to be vigilant no matter how wearing the journey. Gideon's journey would be even more wearing, with the prospect of cannon fire at the end of it. At least at the end of her journey, she'd see her mother. That thought buoyed her spirits.

She'd heard so little from home in the years she'd been gone. She'd written letters home, but she had no idea how many of them had actually found their way to her mother's hands. At least one, for a return letter had found Heather in Virginia. The thin page of writing was now tattered from many readings. Just the sight of her mother's handwriting had been a comfort during those summer months when even the sight of food brought on a green sickness. Once she was sure of what the nausea meant, she'd written her mother, telling her the news while still hiding it from Gideon. She liked to imagine the smile on her mother's face when she read that she was to be a grandmother. A smile Heather was looking forward to seeing in person not so long from now.

When at last the train jerked to a stop in Danville, Heather stood and stretched. Her back ached as if she'd scrubbed a hundred uniforms. She clutched her valise close against her and waited for the light-headedness to fade away. She stepped off the train and looked around at the people going about their business.

How she wished someone was there to meet her, but she'd had no time to send word of her coming. Here and there she spotted a familiar face, but none she could call a name. Nor did any call out to her. Her father had never been much for going into the town, and when he did, he sometimes took her brother Simon but never Heather or the younger children.

They went to the church not far from their home when no need on the farm kept them away and sometimes joined the neighbors for hog killings or quilting bees. Then the near neighbors, the Fentons, made sorghum every year, an event that drew people from miles around. That's where she'd first met Gideon. No sweeter day lived in Heather's memory.

Her mouth watered at the thought of that sorghum and some freshly churned butter on her mother's biscuits. She pulled her wrap closer about her and, after stopping to buy cheese and bread, started up the road, eating as she went. With the sun sliding across the sky toward the western horizon, she began to worry night might overtake her before she reached the farm.

While she'd slept out many the night since she'd left home, that was with Gideon beside her and an army surrounding her. Things were different with no one standing between her and whatever dangers might lurk in the darkness. There could be wolves or even a bear, though she'd never heard of one near home. More likely the wolves and bears she needed most to fear were the two-legged kind. Even so, she walked on. The thought of her mother looking up and seeing her come in the door was enough to give her energy to keep going. A prodigal daughter come home. Heather let the Bible story of the prodigal son play through her mind.

She had left home, but not like the son in the story who had squandered his money. Heather had left with nothing but a change of clothes and a few coins her mother had tied into a handkerchief and pressed into her hands. Now she had a bit more money. The velvet bag containing her army earnings bounced against her breast as she walked down the road. She'd hidden it away in the bodice of her dress after the worry of someone grabbing her valise had kept her awake on the train.

She looked back over her shoulder with some regret that she hadn't stopped to buy a piece of cloth for her mother and some penny candy for her sister and little brothers. But she'd left the town behind.

A farmer stopped his team beside her and let her climb up on the hay in his wagon. He didn't seem interested in conversation, keeping his eyes forward, and she was just as glad. She lay back on the hay and gave herself over to the wagon's bounces as she thought again of her mother's table that might hold supper soon.

Her father at the head with Jimmy in the small one's chair. Jimmy had been only two when Heather left, so he might not even remember her. Then there was little Lucas and Willie and dear Beth, who would be sixteen now. Simon wouldn't be there, but it would be so good to have her young brothers' arms around her, to see Beth's sweet smile, to hear her mother's laugh and feel her lips on her cheek. She'd had to go with Gideon, but that didn't mean she never thought to return.

The sun was going down when she recognized a path through the field as a shortcut to home and called to the farmer to stop. She stood in the roadway and thanked the old man for the ride.

The wide brim of his straw hat shadowed his wrinkled face, but it didn't hide his concern.

"It don't seem right to leave you here alone, missy." He flicked his eyes to her face and then back to ground. "Not in your condition."

"Where I'm going is just across the way." She pointed toward the stand of trees between her and the house and then looked at the sun slipping below the horizon. "I'll be there before nightfall."

He looked toward the trees and his concern became a frown. "Things have been hard around here lately. The cholera came to visit late in the summer, you know."

"No, I didn't know." Cholera. The very word was enough to chill her heart.

"Carried off my daughter-in-law. That's what brought me and the wife to these parts to help our son with his young'uns until he can find another wife." His eyes touched on Heather again. "You wouldn't happen to be returning home a widow, would you?"

Her worst fears put into words. Suddenly light-headed again, she held to the side of the wagon as she forced out an answer. "No."

"Didn't mean to upset you, ma'am, but this war has turned many a young woman into a widow. I thought that might be why you were headed home."

"I've been with my husband's unit as a washerwoman, but a battlefield is hardly a proper place for our child to take his first breath."

"Not a proper place for any child." Sadness sounded in his words.

"You have a boy in the war?" Heather asked.

"The younger one. We've not heard from him in months. I fear we never will." The man blew out a long breath of air before he went on. "Don't let my worry be yours. The fighting can't go on much longer."

"I pray it is so." Heather stepped away from the wagon.

He picked up the reins. "I won't ask which color he wears. Best not to know. Let us part neighbors, not enemies." He looked off at the trees beside the road again. "If you be sure you can make it safe from here, my supper is calling."

He watched her off the road and then flicked the reins to make his horses begin plodding on toward their supper too.

Each tree in the woods was like an old friend as she rushed along the familiar path. Toward home. The only thing that could make it better was Gideon hurrying along beside her instead of marching south to engage the enemy. At the same time, she couldn't quite forget the farmer talking about cholera. She shook her head a little. She didn't have to worry about that now. That dreaded disease brought death only in the warmer seasons. The November air was chill. So chill she wished for mittens for her hands. The coldest part of winter would soon be upon them.

Dusk had fallen before she came out of the trees to see the house across the field. The cow was in the lot next to the barn. The milking through. The chickens would be on their roosts. Even the dogs, Ring and Star, would be curled for the night on the porch.

She stopped and studied the sight of the house. The only house she'd known since there'd been nothing but camps after she left with Gideon. The place looked different somehow. Smaller, shabbier, with wood stacked high on the front porch. They'd never kept wood on the front porch. The roof looked to be sagging in the middle, as if the weight of the wood was pulling at it. She'd been gone two years. Houses aged the same as people. And it had been foolish of her to expect flowers, even if that was the picture she carried in her head. The simple house brightened by her mother's flowers. Her mother had a way with flowers, but there could be no flowers until spring.

The two hounds didn't bark until the squeak of the front gate roused them. The dogs scrambled up to come barreling down off the porch, their barks ringing in the air. She spoke their names, and with her remembered voice in their ears, they silenced and pranced toward her with tails wagging.

4

*T*he dogs licked her hands, giving her a welcome home that brought a smile to her face as she moved toward the house with them bumping against her legs.

"Who goes there?" Her father's voice boomed out from the porch. None of the dogs' welcome sounded in it.

Heather kept her hand on Ring's head and peered up at her father. Enough light lingered that she knew he recognized her before she spoke. "It's me, Father. Heather."

She spoke her name plainly, in hopes her mother would come to the door and run down off the porch to embrace her. Her father made not the first step toward her nor did a smile crease his face. She looked past him to where Beth and two of her little brothers peeked out the door, but she saw no sign of her mother. Heather's heart began to pound up in her ears, and the baby kicked frantically.

"So is he dead?" Her father's voice was cold. "Like your brother Simon."

Simon dead? The words were like fists slamming into her heart. Dear Simon, her friend and playmate through all their young years.

His face flashed through her memory. His father's favorite, but never like him. A boy with a ready smile and a generous heart.

"Well, have you no answer?" her father demanded. At the sound of his voice, the dogs lowered their heads and slunk away to hide under the porch.

She pulled in a breath and managed to speak. "Gideon was alive when last I saw him."

She stared up at her father with a nameless fear awakening in her heart to join the sorrow of knowing Simon was dead. Where was her mother? Her mouth went dry from more than the need of a drink. She dreaded putting the question to her father, for the answer seemed to be written in the lines of his face. Grief sat heavy there. But that could be for Simon. Perhaps her mother was only ill or caring for a sick neighbor. She wouldn't think of the old farmer speaking of cholera.

"Then what are you doing here? A Yankee camp follower." The words came out like a curse.

"I came home to let my mother help me birth my baby." She put her hands on her stomach as though to protect her child from his anger. "Where is she? Will you not let me see my mother?"

He did not answer at once, merely stared at her, but behind him, Beth put her fist against her lips. Young Lucas leaned on Beth and Willie looked down at the floor. That told Heather the truth she dreaded to hear.

"You came too late." The sorrow was plain in her father's voice. "You can do naught but visit her grave now. Buried the two of them together."

"Mother and Simon? He came home before he died?"

"Don't be dense." Her father jerked his head in disgust. "Simon lies buried at Gettysburg with the many others who fell with him at that battle. It's little Jimmy who lies with his mother."

The words came out harsh, but Heather could see the pain they caused him. A pain that shot from him to stab into her. Her head began to spin and she couldn't draw in enough air though she was breathing fast. She reached for something to steady herself, but nothing was near. Only the darkness of the truth poking her from all sides. The cholera had beaten her home.

Through the grainy black creeping over her mind came her father's voice with more pain. "If you'd been here to nurse them, they might even now still be breathing."

Behind him, Beth spoke up, but she sounded miles away to Heather. "Pa, what could Heather have done against the cholera?"

"She started the rent that tore our family apart." Some of the anger came back to strengthen her father's voice as he glared out toward Heather. "You did it. Running away with that Yankee traitor, grieving your mother until she had no strength to fight the sickness. And now you come creeping home expecting an open door to await you."

"I did so hope." The words came out as a whisper, hope in them yet. A hope that was trickling away. What would she do? With her head feeling as if it might float away, she sank to her knees.

"Your hope is misplaced."

From her knees, he looked taller, an immovable force between her and the door. Her and her family. Beth, Willie, and Lucas were staring past him with eyes wide and frightened. They could not go against him.

"You wouldn't turn your own daughter away with nowhere to go? I carry your grandchild." She would beg if she must.

"I have no daughter but one named Beth. You spurned me as father when you went with the army that killed my son. You'll find no place within this house."

Night had fallen while they talked, and she could no longer clearly see his face with the lamplight flowing out the door behind him. He was just a dark shadow ready to engulf her. She bent her head in defeat. What more was there to say?

He turned and went back into the house, herding Willie and Lucas in front of him. Beth slipped past him to run down the porch steps. She bent to touch her cheek to Heather's. "Wait in the barn. I'll come to you there."

"Beth, come into the house." Their father's voice brooked no disobedience as he held open the door. "Now."

She let her hand slide softly across Heather's cheek before she ran back up on the porch to disappear through the door. Her father pulled it closed with a thud.

Heather stared at the door. Her mother gone. Her brothers, Simon and Jimmy, gone. Her hope of home gone. Perhaps Gideon gone too after the coming battles in Tennessee. The darkness pushed at her from inside and out. She wanted to give in to it, sink down on the ground, and let the chill of the night soak into her bones. Perhaps catch the grippe and be done with sorrow. But then the baby was kicking, needing her even more than she had needed the sight of her mother.

The dogs came back out from under the porch when she stood up. She was glad for their company as she headed toward the barn. Something the same from her memories of home. She held the barn door wide to let them come inside with her.

It was dark in the barn, and she had no lantern, no candle, no hope. The mingled smells of dirt, hay, and cows rose up to her, and without bidding, Gideon's face was in her mind. She'd once sneaked out to meet him in this very barn. It had been the deep of the night, but Gideon dispelled the darkness with his kiss.

"The good Lord planned for us to meet and fall in love, my Heather Lou. Of that, I'm certain." He had wrapped his arms around her. "We won't let your father steal our hope of happiness. Nor the war either. Will you do me the honor of being my wife?"

Her heart leaped at his words, and whatever the cost, only one answer had been on her tongue. When she returned to the house, her mother was waiting. Not with condemning words. Without any words at all, she lit a taper and studied Heather's face for a long moment before she blew out the flame.

"I love him," Heather spoke into the dark air that settled between them.

"I cannot turn your father's mind in his favor." Her mother's words were laced with sorrow. "Not while the war's dark cloud is over us."

"I know."

With her hands on Heather's shoulders, she leaned toward her until their faces were inches apart. Love shone in her mother's eyes. She spoke in a whisper, as though she feared the words might seep through the night to Heather's father's ears, but the words carried force nevertheless. "Then do what you must do. The Lord will go with you. As will I. Nothing can ever separate me from your heart. Nothing."

Do what you must do. Heather had done so then, leaving her home to follow Gideon. She would do so now. She was wrong that she had no hope. Just as her mother would ever live within her heart, hope lived within her in the heart of the child she carried.

As her eyes adjusted to the dark, she made out the shapes of the stalls. She knew the barn. She needed no lantern to find her way and Ring stayed close to her side to guide her. He had always been her favorite. She found a box to sit on and the two dogs settled at her feet with satisfied huffs of breath. She had no idea how long it might be before Beth could sneak out to her or even if she would. But there was nothing to do except wait for daybreak. Wait and worry. What was she going to do? She had a little money, but would it be enough to keep her until the war was through?

A few words of Scripture popped into her head. *The Lord directeth his steps.* Pray that the Lord would direct her steps as well. Show her a way. She pulled her cape closer around her. She was cold and hungry. She moistened her dry lips and thought about the spring behind the house. She imagined the cool water in the cup of her hands, but she didn't trust her footing down the incline to the spring in the dark. Better to be thirsty than to risk a fall on the rocks with no one to help her.

No one to help her. The thought chased through her mind over and over until she put her hands on her head and pressed down to stop it. The Lord would help her. She just didn't know how yet.

She leaned back against the barn wall and wondered how long she could go without sleep before she became too weary to walk. She was nodding off when the creak of the barn door brought her upright, her heart pounding. The dogs raised their heads but didn't bark.

"Heather?" her sister called. When Heather didn't answer right away, Beth went on. "Please, be here. We so want to see you."

5

We?" Heather pushed herself up off the wooden box and peered around the post toward the door.

"Lucas is with me. Father's asleep, but Willie stayed behind to warn us if he wakes. He has been such a help to me since Mother . . ." Beth's voice trailed away as she looked around. "Where are you?"

"I'm here." She stepped away from the wall out where they could see her in the bit of moonlight creeping through the open door behind them.

Lucas ran to grab her around the waist, but at the feel of her rounded stomach, hugged very gently. "I was scared I might never see you again," he whispered. "Like Simon. Beth says he's gone the same as Mama and little Jimmy, even if we didn't get to lay him to rest."

Heather ran her hand through his dark, curly hair. Such a familiar feel that tears sprang to her eyes. She had often been the one to see Lucas to bed at night and comb his hair in the mornings after little Jimmy pushed him out of her mother's lap. "How tall you've grown." She leaned over and kissed the top of his head.

"I'm seven now. Big enough to do lots of things, Beth says."

"He is." Beth's voice had a smile in it. "Now let me hug my sister."

Lucas moved back to let the sisters embrace, but he kept his hand on Heather's sleeve.

"You've grown too, Beth," she whispered. "You're not a little girl anymore." She pushed her back to look her over in the dim light.

"I'm almost seventeen."

"And she has a feller," Lucas put in. "Pa's not too happy about that. Neither are me and Willie."

Beth turned toward the boy. "I told you, Lucas, that I won't leave you. Not until you're older. And Pa likes Perry fine."

"Not like Gideon," Heather said.

"No, not like Gideon," Beth echoed her words. "But I'm glad Gideon is all right." She reached over to almost shyly touch Heather's skirt. "Mother got your letter about the baby. She was so happy she couldn't stop smiling."

"What happened to her?" Heather pushed out the question. She had to know, but somehow talking about it made it too real. She wanted it not to be real. To instead be some sort of horrible mistake, but her father's angry words echoed in her head. *She started the rent that tore our family apart.*

"I'll tell you, but first food." Beth pulled a jar of water out of her jacket and biscuits and ham out of her apron pocket. "It's not much, but I didn't want to chance waking Pa."

Heather tried not to grab the water, but she hadn't been so thirsty since they'd marched across Virginia in the August heat. She let the water fill her mouth and swallowed slowly. It would not be good to gulp it down and have it all heave back out if her stomach decided to be unsettled.

"Thank you, Beth. And Lucas too." She smiled at the boy and touched his head again. A shiver went through her from the cool water.

"You're cold," Beth said. "Where's the blanket, Lucas?"

"I must have dropped it." Lucas sounded near tears.

"Worry not. Your company has warmed my heart."

"You still need the blanket." Beth looked toward the door. "Look. Ring has found it and thinks you gave it to him for his bed. Get him off it before he infests it with fleas." Beth laughed as Lucas pushed the dog off the blanket. The sound lightened the darkness better than the moonlight sliding through the cracks between the barn's boards.

"Ring merely warmed it up for me." Heather was surprised to feel a smile taking root inside her too as Beth draped the blanket around her. The warmth was more than welcome.

They settled back in the middle room of the barn. It was darker there, but she knew their faces. Now she needed to know their story. She swallowed the biscuit and ham and could not keep back the thought of her mother's biscuits she'd imagined eating earlier. She wrapped the last biscuit in the cloth napkin and shoved it in her pocket, her appetite and any thought of laughter gone. "Tell me about Mother."

Beth sighed and was quiet a long moment before she began speaking, sorrow plain in her voice. "A week after she got your letter back the first of September, Jimmy got sick. At first we thought maybe he'd caught a chill playing in the creek. You remember how Jimmy loved splashing in the water. But thinking back, I believe Mother feared the worst from the very beginning. Pa had heard talk of the cholera in town. She took Jimmy in her bedroom and wouldn't let any of us come in until she was too sick to raise her head. I had to take care of them then. I had to. Jimmy died first. Then Mother. I figured I'd go next, but the Lord spared me."

"Oh, Beth, our father was right. I should have been here to help you." Heather grasped Beth's hand as Lucas tried to hug them both.

"You couldn't have stopped the cholera. Nobody can do that. Pa knows that. He just can't think straight right now what with all the dying. Can't none of us."

"He's not going to change his mind about me." It was best to face the truth of that.

29

"No," Beth agreed. "Mother might have been able to convince him, but I can't tell him anything. Me or the boys. But he does love the boys. Losing Simon tore him apart even before the sickness took Mother and Jimmy."

Lucas must have noted how Beth didn't include herself in the circle of their father's love. He grabbed Beth's hand and declared, "I love you. Willie and me, we both love you." He turned to look at Heather. "And you too. No matter what Pa says."

Heather touched his cheek. "You were always a tenderhearted boy. You must have taken that after our mother."

"He is much like her," Beth agreed. "Willie's more like Pa, ready to fight the world sometimes."

"Thirteen can be a hard age for boys," Heather said. "They always want to be older."

"I'm glad he's not." Beth's voice was firm. "He'd have run after Simon to the army if he'd had a few more years, but now they say the war's the same as over. That the Yankees have won." Beth peered over at Heather. "You were with them. So, is that true?"

"The fighting hasn't stopped, but so many have died and those still standing are weary of war. I have no way of knowing, but I think, I pray it will end soon."

"How was it? Following the army?" Beth asked.

"Not easy. I had no idea what would happen when I left home. I just knew I wanted to be with Gideon. I guess I was lucky to get the washerwoman job since it meant I got to stay near Gideon, but I paid for it by seeing sights no girl should ever see. There were times I wondered if the Lord had tired of our sinfulness and was bringing down a flood of artillery to wipe us out. But then the guns would stop firing and Gideon would come back in one piece and life went on with more trousers to wash."

Heather paused, but neither Beth nor Lucas spoke. So she went on. "Then I got in the family way and Gideon didn't want our baby born on a battlefield."

Beth reached over to touch the swell of Heather's stomach. "When is your time of confinement?"

"Late December as near as I can figure."

"A Christmas baby," Lucas spoke up.

"Perhaps." A smile tugged at Heather's lips, but it didn't last. She clutched her hands in her lap and looked toward her sister. "What am I going to do, Beth? I came home to Mother and now she's gone."

"She didn't forget you at the end." Beth pulled something out of her pocket. The paper captured the scant light in the barn. "I suppose she had a prescience of things to come. She thought you might come home, so when she took sick, she wrote this to you."

Heather reached for it and held it to her heart. Her mother's last thoughts of her. Tears pushed at her eyes, but she held them in. Lucas and Beth had seen enough tears. After a moment she opened the page, but she could only see the shape of the letter. "I have no light to read the words."

"You'll have to wait until morning," Beth said. "I couldn't take the chance of Pa seeing us cross the yard with a lantern. But Mother bade me read it. I can tell you what it says if you want."

"Do." Heather folded the letter and held it to her cheek as though she could absorb the written words while Beth spoke them aloud.

"She writes that if you have a need that cannot be met here at home, to go to Aunt Sophrena."

"Aunt Sophrena?" Heather frowned.

"You remember Mother speaking of her, don't you? Our grandfather's younger sister. Sophrena. Such a pretty name that I've always wondered about her."

"But we've never met her. She went to the Shakers before I was born." Why would her mother pick that aunt? There were other family members. None close by, but neither was the Shaker village. That was in the next county.

"True enough, but she wrote to Mother last year before Christmas and Mother wrote back. Pa didn't like it. He says those Shaker

31

people only pretend to be upright and holy and no telling what goes on there." Beth looked at Lucas, whose head was drooping. "I should have left Lucas in bed."

"I'm so glad you didn't." Heather eased the boy's head over into her lap and stroked his hair. "Touching him thus has been reward enough for my long walk home even if I must leave straightway in the morning."

"I wish it could be otherwise, but Pa won't relent. Before light you must go into the woods. I'll send Willie out with more food when he comes out to milk the cow. Then you'll have to go to Perry's house."

"Are you talking about Perry Wilson? Is that your fellow?" Heather remembered a kid always making a pest of himself.

As if Beth guessed her thoughts, she said, "He's grown up the same as me. You remember where his house is, don't you?"

"I remember."

"Good. He'll take you to the Shaker village."

Beth had it all figured out. Arranged and decided, but Heather wasn't as sure. "I can't go live among the Shakers. I'm married with child. That's against their beliefs."

"After Mother passed, I read Aunt Sophrena's letters. She has a kind spirit. And I have heard the same said about the Shakers by others. They might have odd ways, but they don't turn away those in need."

"But I can't give up Gideon."

"You've already given him up until the war is over, have you not? When he comes home, then you can leave the Shakers and go with him."

Heather stared at Beth. Even in the dim light, she could see the set of her jaw. "You're acting like the elder sister instead of the younger one."

"I have stepped into Mother's shoes. A difficult fit, but I must try to wear them anyway. So listen to our mother's words coming through me. The Shakers will treat you kindly. When you read

Mother's letter at first light, you will see it's the best way right now. The only way. The Shakers don't take part in war. According to Aunt Sophrena, they seek peace above all else. Simple peace."

Heather tucked the letter inside her bodice before reaching across the dozing Lucas to grasp Beth's hand. "I so wish I could stay and help you."

"So do I, but Pa won't accept a Yankee into his house. Not while the wound of Simon's death is so fresh in his mind."

"I'm not a Yankee. I'm his daughter."

"And my sister. Nothing can ever change that." Beth squeezed her hand before shaking Lucas to wake him. "Come, little brother. Give Heather another hug before we must go as quietly as shadows back to our beds."

They clung to each other for a long moment. Then Beth and Lucas slipped silently out the barn door. The two dogs followed after them, leaving Heather far too alone. She pulled the blanket tight around her to keep in every bit of warmth and tried to imagine what this aunt Sophrena might look like. Stiff. Stern. Still, the Shakers did dance to worship. That did not sound so stiff. It sounded amazingly odd. The very thought made Heather's head spin, but she did have one clear thought. There was no way Heather could ever be a Shaker. Not if she had to give up Gideon or her baby.

Would the Shakers ask her to do that? Heather reached up to feel the crackle of her mother's letter under her dress and, in spite of her weariness, wished for the morning light.

6

Sophrena Prescott arose from bed at the first toll of the Shaker rising bell the way she had for the last twenty-five years. Habits clung to her like lint to a dark cloak. The other sisters in the room were also getting out of bed at the sound of the bell.

Time to be up and the day to begin. Chores awaited. Beds to make. Floors to sweep. Biscuits to cook. She had kitchen duty. Not a bad duty for November when the warmth of the ovens was welcome instead of suffocating the way it was in the summer months.

She knelt by her bed for the morning prayer. The other sisters in the room were doing the same. Sophrena could almost feel the silent prayers rising around her as they welcomed the day and gave thanks for the blessing of work and the love of God. Hands to work, hearts to God. The words slipped through her mind like a needle through worn cloth. But words alone did not make a proper prayer any more than a needle by itself could mend a rip in a garment. One had need of thread knotted to hold the stitches. Prayers had need of a connection to the heart.

Forgive me, Lord. She pushed the words silently toward the heavenly Father. Truly the most sincere prayer words she'd offered in days. But for what did she beg forgiveness? She had no outward sins. She continued her Shaker walk without visible fault. The faults were in the weariness of her thinking. Her fault was in losing her joy. Her proper joy. The joy of a covenanted Believer.

She'd signed the Covenant of Belief many years ago and become a Shaker in heart and mind. While she'd been resistant when she and her husband in the world had first come to the Shakers, once at Harmony Hill, she'd found the village had much to offer. Decidedly more than marriage to a man with no love for her in spite of the marriage vows they'd spoken.

Strange how things worked out. Jerome, the one enthused by the idea of Shaker life, had not persevered. Instead he had left the Believers and gone back to the world. He had not asked her to go with him. He had not asked her anything, but merely freed himself from the worldly ties of marriage by getting a divorce on the grounds that she was a Shaker. A reason the courts in Kentucky accepted without argument. It mattered not that he was the reason she had become a Shaker in the first place.

Sophrena had no argument with it either. In fact, she'd paid it little note. By then, she was part of a larger family. She was Sister Sophrena and content in the company of her Shaker sisters and brothers. She willingly worked at whatever task she was assigned and in time was entrusted with the guidance of the younger sisters. Oh, how she loved her little sisters as she gently prodded them along the Shaker path, but perhaps even more she had liked recording those journeys in the family's journal. A visible record of the village activities.

She pulled her dress on, draped her collar around her neck, and tied on her apron. She tried not to think about the feel of the pen in her hand as words spilled from her to dance across the page. No more. Some years before, the Ministry had decided she was not keeping her journal entries properly simple in reporting the doings of the family and had given that task over to others.

'Tis a gift to be simple, Sophrena reminded herself as she adjusted her cap. Some of the sisters were taking turns at the small mirror to situate their caps properly, but Sophrena had no need of a looking glass to position her cap. It settled on her head like the old friend it was. Like the pen had once fit in her hand.

A sigh whispered through her. She kept her eyes away from Sister Betty, who now had the task of recording the happenings of their West family each day. She would not allow envy to creep into her mind. What difference did it make that Sister Betty's reports were as dry as broom straw left out in the sunshine all the good days of fall? Dry was good for broom straw. And approved for journals.

Sophrena had no problem imagining how Sister Betty's entry would read for this day. *November 21, 1864. The kitchen sisters baked 5 dozen biscuits, 25 loaves of bread, peeled and boiled a bushel of potatoes. The weather was fine. No one made a new pattern for the chair bottoms. The men shucked corn, fed the cattle, built a fence. Everything was the same, the very same as November 20 was and as November 22 will be.*

With a shake of her head to clear away her foolish thoughts, she descended the stairs two floors to the kitchen to make those five dozen biscuits. The other sisters assigned to kitchen duty glanced up from their work to welcome her with smiles and a quiet greeting. Each had her task, so there was no need for useless chatter.

The same was good, she sternly told herself as she measured out the flour and baking soda. Unity was the pathway to peace. One had no need for upsetting thoughts when one knew each step that would be taken in a day's time. A month's time. A year's time. There was no need for words on a page to speak of a yearning in the heart for something more. Such words would do naught but plummet her into sin. It was good she was no longer entrusted with record keeping. Surely it was a vanity to be so taken with one's own words that one desired them visible in front of one's eyes.

She dumped the dough out of the wooden bowl onto the flour-dusted biscuit board and began rolling it out to the proper thickness. With no wasted motions, she cut the biscuits and lined them up on the baking pans. Dozens of biscuits. The brothers would be hungry. The sisters would be hungry. The children would be hungry. No children would be eating Sophrena's biscuits here in this house. The children were in the children's house, but some sister there would be in the kitchen rolling out biscuit dough and using a like biscuit cutter to make the biscuits. Every family dwelling in the village would have a sister doing the same.

The same. Everything was the same. Why could she no longer take comfort from that sameness?

She mashed down the remains of the dough and rolled it out again. Nothing was to be wasted. A Shaker was a good steward of her blessings. A good Shaker didn't question why the dough must be rolled out an inch thick. A good Shaker understood that such things were learned by many like hands rolling out biscuits and that experience shared by the Ministry to all Shaker kitchens. One had no reason to wonder if a thin biscuit might taste better on this day.

Sophrena folded the biscuit dough back together to make the proper thickness. A thin biscuit would bake up too hard and end up useless crumbles on the plates of her brothers and sisters. Was that what was wrong with her? Had she somehow rolled her spirit out too thin and now it was crumbling under too much contrary thinking?

She tried to concentrate only on the task at hand. The mixing of the dough. The cutting of the biscuits. But the chore took no thought and her mind would not be silenced on this morning. A reason for her discontent must be found so she could whirl it away when next they had meeting.

Another sigh escaped her lips. She was glad for the kitchen clatter that kept her sisters from noting it. But in truth, there had been many meetings, many chances to whirl away her wrong thinking, and her feet had moved through the dances by rote, feeling nothing at all. Even there in the meetinghouse, her spirit lay flat and useless within her.

"Sister Sophrena, you don't seem yourself this day." Sister Edna stepped up beside Sophrena, the corners of her mouth turned down in fake concern.

Sophrena composed her face. She had no desire to share her discontent with Sister Edna, who had no concern for anything except proving herself more faithful and more worthy than her sisters. What she lacked was more kindness. She seemed to rejoice when one of the sisters stumbled. No doubt she would celebrate if Sophrena was tripped up by the malaise spreading through her.

"It has been a long year," Sophrena said. "With much sorrow. It wears on one knowing the world outside our village borders is in upheaval with armies of neighbors shooting and killing one another."

"You should not listen to the news if it is going to send you into a season of melancholy." Sister Edna's eyes, never very wide, narrowed even more as she looked at Sophrena. "Besides, the war has nothing to do with us. We do not pick up weapons of destruction."

"Yea," Sophrena agreed. "But all are not Believers. Surely you remember the echo of cannons from a few years ago when the armies met at nearby Perryville intent on destroying one another. Each blast meant mayhem and death. Such is still going on even if our ears can no longer hear the noise."

"I well remember that time and a sorry time it was." A frown flashed across Sister Edna's face. "Those soldiers coming through here like locusts eating our food. We did nothing but cook day and night for too many days to name. I feared we would starve come winter."

"Our food stores are plentiful now. It has been a good harvest." Sophrena regretted speaking of the war to Sister Edna. She was sorry of the necessity of speaking anything to Sister Edna, but such was not acceptable thinking. She managed more words. "We can feed any who come."

"As our Mother Ann instructs. Turn none in need away."

"It is good to have a generous heart." Sophrena agreed in hopes Sister Edna would be satisfied and turn back to her own kitchen tasks. There was nothing generous about the sister's heart. Or seemingly, her own this morn.

Even now, she sensed Sister Edna was seeking the proper words to be sure Sophrena realized which of them had the better spirit. Sophrena didn't care. They had long been sisters together here at Harmony Hill. They were to have love for one another. It was so ordered, but proper love could not always be forced into one's heart. Some sisters were harder to see kindly than others. Sophrena started to turn away from Sister Edna to check on the biscuits. She had no need to hear more of her words. Or to reveal any more of her own malaise to this sister. It was Eldress Lilith who must hear Sophrena's confessions of wrongs done, whether of thought or deed.

"Perhaps the Ministry should forbid you to receive mail if it is going to cause you to surrender to worries of the world," Sister Edna said. "Just as they forbade you to write in your journal when it was noted you were straying from the proper path of simple living."

"Perhaps so," Sophrena murmured without looking at Sister Edna. She pulled the first tray of biscuits out of the oven, taking no care to keep the pan from clanging against the oven sides. She hoped to attract the attention of Sister Nora, whose duty it was to keep all on task in the kitchen, but she did not seem bothered by the noise or the needless chatter.

So Sophrena turned and looked directly at Sister Edna. "The bell will soon toll for us to carry the food to the dining area. I must see to my tasks." Sophrena let a ghost of a smile touch her lips. "As I am sure you must as well."

"You needn't worry about me faithfully performing my duty, Sister Sophrena." Sister Edna's voice lost any hint of warmth as she glared at her. "It is you who appears to be in need of proper attention to your tasks. It's ever been so since you let that former sister step too close to you. The Ministry should have barred every memory of her from our village instead of allowing her letters to you. Now I hear she's sent you a book with her name upon it. Why ever did they not send it back at once?"

"That is a question best asked of the Ministry. It is not my place to try to divine their thoughts." Sophrena should have let the matter rest there, but she could not. Their former sister had ever been a splinter of discord between the two of them. Sister Edna had resented Jessamine's lack of discipline while Sophrena had loved the young girl's joyful enthusiasm for life. "She has been gone from us for fifteen years. Perhaps they have forgiven her leaving and are merely pleased she has found a place in the world writing stories."

"Foolishness. That's what it is." Sister Edna pushed her hand through the air in dismissal. "Naught but foolishness."

"Nevertheless, stories those of the world seem fond of, from all reports," Sophrena said mildly. "Our former sister seems to do well in the world."

"No one does well in the world. Have you forgotten its evil actions and sorrow?" Sister Edna let out a disgusted huff. "Especially out there in the wild state of California. That is where she went, is it not?"

"Yea, you are right, my sister." Sophrena began lifting the biscuits off the pan to put into the baskets. Eight in each basket to be set in the middle of four sisters or four brethren so there would be no need for talk as they took care of the serious business of feeding their bodies.

She could feel Sister Edna staring at her still, but she continued her task as she wished there was a rule against talking in the kitchen as well as the dining area. The bell would signal the morning meal soon, and while she might not be taking the proper joy in her work, she did intend to accomplish it as expected. She was relieved when Sister Edna blew out another disgusted breath and picked up a stack of plates to go set the tables.

Was Sister Edna right? Were the letters she had received from those in the world upsetting her peace? Not the letters from Jessamine. They were always reason for joy. Just thinking about Jessamine brought a smile to Sophrena's lips even in the midst of her malaise.

On the other hand, the letters from her family in the world were reason for sadness. She had no idea why she had reached out to her worldly family after so many years of being the same as dead to them. The Believers were her family, and yet the desire had awakened in her to know what had become of her worldly family. In so doing, she opened her heart to grief. Her brother of the world's daughter, Susan, wrote back to share her deep sadness over the loss of her son at Gettysburg.

It would have been cruel to not respond to such an evident plea for someone to listen to her sorrow. For a year the letters had flown between them, with Sophrena coming to know the family through Susan's words. The stress was there in their small family just as Mother Ann warned it would be, but something else was there too that pulled at Sophrena's heart.

Then a couple of months ago a letter had come in a different hand. That of Susan's young daughter reporting the cholera had taken her mother and her youngest brother. Life was so fragile. It was good to be insulated here in the Shaker village. Yet, at the same time, Sophrena was beginning to wonder if there was more. She'd turned fifty before the coming of spring. She told herself it mattered not how old she was, but at the same time a strange desire arose in her to experience more of life. To know what it was to love as the world loved. As Susan and her family loved.

Sophrena brushed her hand across her forehead as if she could wipe away such wayward thoughts. Why now, at her age, would the forbidden fruit suddenly look so tempting? And why with the season of joy coming upon them when they celebrated the birth of Christ?

But first there would be Sacrifice Day, a day of atonement. Perhaps that would get her spirit back in order the way the use of a broom and a dusting brush could get a room back into fit shape for use. On that day, a leader from the New Lebanon village was expected to help them focus their prayers on righting their spirits and regaining unity with their Shaker brothers and sisters. Sacrifice Day could not come too soon for Sophrena.

7

"What's the matter with you, Worth?" Jake White crouched down beside the little fire Gideon had coaxed to life. "You lost your smile?"

"Hard to smile on a day like this." Gideon rubbed his arms to warm them. The cold drizzle that had fallen all day was freezing in the air now that the sun was gone.

"You've got a fire." Jake held his hands out toward the promise of heat from the flames. "That's something of a miracle on this wet day. And welcome it is. Our tents will be coated in ice come morning or I miss my guess."

The flames spluttered in the damp air before bravely flickering back up. Gideon stared at his coffeepot on the fire as though he could will it to heat faster. His back was wet. The skin between his toes was rotting, and he wasn't sure he'd kept his gun dry. What good did it do a man to march to battle if he didn't even know whether his gun would fire?

The tents stretched out over the flat expanse of a farmer's field littered with cow pies, but no cows were in evidence now. Farmers had a way of making their herds disappear when an army was coming through. Gideon shut his eyes and imagined beef sizzling on a spit over his fire. But there was no fresh meat this night. Only hardtack and salt pork.

Gideon fed the fire a little more wood. A cup of coffee might make the night bearable. He was hungry. He was always hungry. He had hardtack. Another reason for the coffee. He needed to dunk the hardtack in it so the weevils would float to the top. He'd eaten the stuff often enough, weevils and all, but he preferred full dark to do that. Even then he felt the little creatures wiggling on his tongue. And here Jake White was, expecting him to smile.

He looked across his struggling fire at Jake. "Tell me, what do you miss the most about home?"

"That's easy enough on a night like this one," Jake said. "Warming my bones by the stove, a blanket around my feet and a hot drink in my hands. Then again, a few months back I guess I would have been wishing for a cool shade by a blue lake. The weather can change a man's mind quick."

"Weather don't matter all that much when somebody's ready to shoot at you."

"You're right there, lad, but you've got to remember you're wanting to shoot back."

"Wanting to? I never wanted to shoot anybody." Gideon speared a piece of salt pork and held it directly in the flames. Grease from the pork caused the fire to flare up and gave him hope for the coffee. He'd gladly exchange the salt pork for a hot cup of coffee.

"But we do. Shoot back." Jake stared at the fire as he pulled some hardtack out of his pocket and bit off a piece without even checking for weevils. "We have to. It's what soldiers do."

"I want to go home, Jake." The meat was shriveling to nothing as grease kept spattering into the fire, but he didn't pull his roasting stick back.

"That's the other thing soldiers do. Think about home." Jake took another bite of the hardtack and chewed awhile before he went on. "Your trouble is you had home with you and now she's gone."

"Gone," he echoed Jake. He pulled his roasting stick back and blew on the crisp of meat the fire hadn't stolen before he ate it off the stick.

"She'll be all right," Jake said after a minute. "The girl marched with us for months without once having the vapors."

"But what if the baby decided to come early? Or who knows what might happen." He poked the stick into the fire.

"True enough, lad. But if it does, it's better for her to be in the bosom of her loving family than here where bullets can start flying." Jake pulled a tin cup from his pack and held it out. "Let's give that coffee a try if you've got a wee bit to share."

Gideon folded his handkerchief to grasp the coffeepot, lift it from the fire, and pour their cups full. They both took a few sips of the bracing liquid and then dumped their hardtack into their cups. After a few seconds, Gideon held his cup closer to the light of the fire to skim off the weevils that had risen to the top. Then he fished out the hardtack and wished he'd asked Heather to send him a box of sugar cookies. Maybe she would. Maybe the mail would catch up with them after a few weeks. Before Christmas. It would be nice to have a taste of Christmas instead of only hardtack.

"Do you think we'll still be fighting at Christmas?" Gideon asked.

"It's likely. I'm just hoping we're not still fighting come the Christmas after this one."

"But isn't Christmas supposed to be a time of peace?"

"Tell that to the generals. In a war, one day follows another and one soldier runs up the hill after another falls until one side gives up."

"But there are things worth fighting for, aren't there, Jake?" Gideon took another drink of the coffee and was glad for the slightly sweet, yet bitter taste and the warmth it shot through him.

"We aim to keep the Union together." Jake sipped his coffee too. They were both quiet a moment before he went on. "Even if we have to kill our brothers to do it."

"Or let them kill us."

"You're wrong on that, lad. We aren't letting anybody kill us. Certainly not you with a baby on the way." Firelight danced on his face as he leaned toward Gideon. "Think of it, lad. By Christmas, you'll be a father."

"What do I know about being a father?" Gideon stared down into his cup. If weevils still floated there, the darkness blessedly hid them.

"Enough, lad." Jake said. "You'll know enough."

"If I live long enough."

"There is that," Jake said. "The weather don't kill us, the rations might." He threw the dregs of his coffee out on the ground.

After Jake left to go climb into his tent, Gideon stared at the fire and remembered the way Heather looked on that last night they were together. Would he ever feel her head resting on his shoulder again?

8

$\mathcal{T}$he Shaker village surprised Heather. Buildings spread out
from the road, several of them rising high above her as she
rode into the town on Perry's wagon. Some were of hewn stone.
Others brick. Several frame buildings were painted dark orange.
Not at all a color she had expected to see on a Shaker building.

Perry pointed out a white frame building in the center of the village across from a huge white stone building. "That's their church.
They call it a meetinghouse. It's where they dance." He gave the
building a sideways look as if he hoped to see some of that dancing but at the same time was afraid he might. "Pa's seen it and he
says it's mighty strange."

Perry, the same as Beth, had grown up in the last two years.
Now instead of an awkward kid, he was a young man obviously
completely smitten with Beth. That's all he'd wanted to talk about
on the ride to the Shaker village. That and the war. Heather had
to tell him she couldn't talk about the war. The very thought of
Gideon headed toward another battle made her head swim and
she had to grip the wagon seat to keep upright.

She could have told Perry plenty. How she'd been deafened by the cannons and gunfire. That was what Perry wanted to know. He wanted to hear about courageous charges to take a hill, but Heather was tormented by the memory of the men who didn't rise back up after the hill had been taken and would never make a new charge at the enemy. The enemy fell the same on the other side of whatever line the generals determined had to be taken or defended. She'd gone among the wounded men offering them water and been anxious and afraid often enough, but a washerwoman couldn't give in to feminine vapors. At least then she'd known what was happening.

Now she could only imagine and worry. What if Gideon never came home? Whatever would happen to her with no husband and a father who shut his door to her?

She stared up at the Shaker buildings. They took in those in need. That was why she was riding into their village. But she couldn't stay here. Not forever. They divided families. She'd heard her grandmother speak harshly of the way Shakers didn't believe in marriage and had special houses where children were kept from their parents.

Heather put a hand over the swell of her baby inside her. Surely they wouldn't take a newborn from his mother's bosom. Heather's mother couldn't have imagined that happening or she'd have never told her to come find this aunt Sophrena.

Her hand slid over to her mother's letter tucked deep in her pocket. That morning when the night began to cede to the coming day, she'd slipped out of the barn and hurried across the frost-encrusted grass to hide among a stand of trees. She hadn't wanted to chance encountering her father's wrath again by lingering in the barn overlong. The dogs didn't bark at her, nor did they leave their warm spots on the porch to come to her.

Her feet were freezing. Her back ached, and her spirit was weary. She stood there as stiff and cold as the trees and prayed for the morning light to hurry. She didn't know how much longer she could bear the darkness.

"Oh, Mother, I did so need your arms around me," Heather

whispered into the shadows. Tears traced down her cheeks, and she pulled the quilt Lucas had carried out to her tighter around her shoulders.

She ran her hands over the bits of thread knotted through the fabric to keep the batting in place. Her mother's hands had tied those threads. Thinking that gave her some comfort as she unfolded her mother's letter. Fingers of pink were reaching up into the eastern sky, but the writing was still only a dark blur. She stared at the paper anyway and waited for morning to crawl over the horizon and bring light.

The first word she could make out was "Heather." The next, at the bottom of the letter, was "Mother." She held the paper against her heart and tried to absorb the love there as she leaned against the maple she and Simon called their monkey tree. She looked up at the branches and remembered climbing the tree with Simon always climbing a little higher. The memory of their laughter as they perched high above their small world filled her with longing for a happier time. Before the war tore their family apart, everything was good.

She'd cried when Simon shouldered his rifle and went off to war. To the South. She hadn't understood that then. She didn't understand it now. What had pulled them—her father and Simon—to the South? They had no slaves. They spent sunrise to sunset scratching out a meager living from the hard ground.

"A man can't let the government order his life," Simon had told her. "He has to be free."

The word "free" echoed in her head. The slaves had been freed. Lincoln had issued an Emancipation Proclamation. Strange how both sides looked at free from different eyes. And how free was just a word that meant nothing when shells started exploding. On a battlefield, nobody was free. Every person anywhere near could be caught in a web of violence.

What did the Bible say about freedom? That all were shackled by sin and only through Christ could true freedom be found. *Ye shall be free indeed.*

Now her mother and Simon and Jimmy knew that eternal
freedom, but before her mother went to be with the Lord, she'd
remembered Heather. At long last the gray light of dawn crept in
under the trees to let Heather read her mother's words.

My dearest Heather,

*Oh, how it pains my heart to think I will never lay eyes on
you again in this lifetime. Or Simon. Or Jimmy. I will soon be
with them, but you I am leaving behind. You and the sweet
babe you are carrying. My arms ache with longing as I think of
the child forming within you. I so wish to hold that precious
child, a promise of life continuing at a time when death has
stolen so much from us and now knocks on the door for me.*

*But I know you are coming. Not soon enough and I'm
glad of that, for I want you far from this sickness. I weep
each time Beth comes near and pray that when you do come
you will not find all your family in the grave. But enough of
grief. I must save my strength for hope for your tomorrow.*

*Simon's death has embittered your father. I fear he will
not welcome you when you come. If Gideon comes with
you, then I trust the two of you will find your way to a good
life without your father's blessings. But I worry you might
return alone before the war ends. I sense that desire between
the lines of your letter telling me about the baby. And oh,
how I wish my hands could be the hands to catch him as he
comes into the world.*

A tear dripped from Heather's cheek down onto the letter to join
the stain made by her mother's tears. She touched the spot where
the ink was smudged and closed her eyes for a long moment. Then
she blinked away her tears in order to keep reading.

*But it is not to be. I have tried to think of what you must
do if your father's heart hasn't softened by then. And the*

thought that comes to me as if the Lord planted it here in my head is Sophrena. You remember me telling you about my aunt who went to the Shakers. Last year, she wrote to me. I wonder now if that was God's plan. Perhaps he knew the troubles headed our way and tapped Sophrena on the shoulder over there in her Shaker village and made her re-member her family.

Your grandmother often spoke ill of the Shakers for they took her daughter from the family circle, but I've heard oth-ers credit them with much charity. I have never been to the Shaker village, but Sophrena is family even if the Shakers claim to shed their kin in the world. I see in the words of her letters a desire to know us. Perhaps God-given for just this moment in your life. The Lord makes a way for his children.

Her mother's writing became shaky. Heather held the paper closer, but try as she might, she couldn't make out the next words. "Mother, don't hide your thoughts from me now," she whispered. She narrowed her eyes and peered at the scribbled letters and some of the words began to come clear.

So tired. . . . can't stop. . . . more to say.

As if through sheer will her mother's hand grew steadier and her writing became clear once more.

One last thing, my precious daughter. Your father does love you even if you think he does not. The death of his sons has made him rage against God and all he holds responsible, and my death will be another grievous blow for him. Don't allow anger to poison your heart as it is poisoning his. Have compassion. Forgive and love. You must.

Your loving Mother

Heather stared at her mother's final words until they became blurry. How could her mother expect her to keep loving a father who turned her away into the cold night without offering so much as a drink of water? Even the men on the battlefields had more compassion than that for their enemies. Heather frowned down at the letter in her hand. Some things went beyond forgiveness.

She was so cold. In the east, clouds were gathering to steal any promise of warmth from the sun. A gray curl of smoke was rising from the house's chimney, but none of that warmth was for her.

What of the quilt your brother carried to you in the night? Heather heard her mother's voice in her head. *Is there not warmth in it? Warmth put there by my own hands.*

Heather pulled the quilt closer around her and remembered her mother sewing scraps of material together to make their quilts. The thought comforted her.

Then Willie was running from the house toward the barn. Halfway there, he peered back over his shoulder before heading for the trees where she waited, as if he'd gotten a sudden call of nature.

All legs and arms, he must have grown taller so quickly his body hadn't been able to keep up. Beth was right. He was like their father. Even the same wrinkle of worry settled between his dark eyebrows when he spotted Heather beside the maple.

"Thank you, Willie," she said when he handed her the sack of food. "Beth tells me she couldn't make it without your help."

He looked down but not before Heather saw a pleased look flash across his face. He traced a line in the hard dirt with the toe of his shoe. "I don't do that much." His voice was that of a boy becoming a man. "It's just that things is hard right now what with our mother gone and Pa feeling so hard toward everybody."

"You don't?" Heather asked. "Feel hard toward me?"

He looked up, surprise on his face. "You're my sister. Mama said family has to stick together."

"She used to tell me the same. Have you grown too old to give your sister a hug?" Heather set the food down and held out her arms to him.

He stepped into her embrace eagerly enough, but pulled back after a few seconds. "Pa will be heading out to the barn."

"And you wouldn't want him to catch you talking to me." Heather kept her eyes on Willie's face. She would not look toward the house and let Willie think her afraid. She would not.

"He'll get better. Beth says he will. That it takes time."

"He's good to you, isn't he?" Heather kept her voice quiet.

"He lets me go hunting with him." A smile lit up Willie's face, but then he pushed it away as if worried he shouldn't be smiling. "Things will get better with you too once he figures out you didn't have anything to do with Simon getting killed."

"I'm sorry about Simon." Tears pushed at Heather's eyes again. "I wish the dying was over."

Willie peered over at her, his eyes curious. "Did you see a lot of fighting?"

"I saw the results." Heather tried to block the memory of the fallen soldiers from her mind. She had enough death to think about here. "I don't want to talk about the war. I'm away from it now."

"But Gideon's not."

"No, he's not." Heather bit the inside of her lip to keep back tears.

"I like Gideon," Willie said. "Even if he is a Yankee. Mama said no matter which side comes out winning, we'll all have to learn to get along again. You think we can?"

"If Mother said so, then maybe we can. For certain, you and I can."

"And Pa too. You'll see. Beth says we just have to be patient."

Patience. Forgiveness. Heather didn't have time for either one. She had a baby on the way and no home. But it wasn't the fault of the boy in front of her. She reached out and touched his cheek. "Thanks, Willie, for bringing the food."

"I almost forgot." He pulled a note out of his pocket. "Beth says give this to Perry. You remember his house? Just this side of the church. You can cut through the field." Willie pointed to the west. "Not but a couple of fences to climb."

"I remember," Heather said.

"Good." Willie looked down toward her middle, then flashed his eyes back up to her face. "You'll be all right?"

"I'll be all right." She did her best to sound sure of her words as she touched his cheek one last time before he turned and loped across the open space toward the barn.

But she hadn't been sure then and she wasn't any surer now here in the middle of the Shaker village with the Shaker men and women moving briskly along the paths beside the road. All so alike with their heads bent to hide their faces under their hats and bonnets. Even if she could see the women's faces, it wouldn't matter. She had no idea what this aunt Sophrena looked like. She had no idea about anything except how very, very tired she was.

Perry helped her down from the wagon in front of a huge brick building. He looked uneasy as he pointed her toward the door. "They're not as bad as some people say. My ma says they're just people like anybody else. Even if they do have some odd ways of thinking."

She thanked him and watched him climb back up on the wagon to start his horses moving. What choice did she have but to turn and climb the stone steps? The door opened and a somber-faced woman in a gray dress with a large white collar lapped over her bosom waited for her. Heather slipped her hand in her pocket to touch her mother's letter.

"Are you sure about this, Mother?" she muttered under her breath.

The door is open, isn't it? Her mother's voice whispered through her mind.

God's plan. That was what her mother had written in her letter. Heather looked back up at the Shaker woman who didn't smile but did speak a word of greeting. She opened the door wider and Heather passed into the warmth inside.

9

The Ministry is deeply concerned about you, Sister Sophrena."
Eldress Lilith folded her hands together on the table between
them and studied Sophrena's face.

Sophrena wasn't sure if it was concern or pity she saw on the
woman's face. The new eldress was so very young. Nothing like
dear Eldress Freda who had stepped over into heaven last year,
taking her wisdom and gentle spirit with her.

Not that Eldress Lilith wasn't wise. Sophrena was sure she was,
else the Ministry would not have raised her to the position of
eldress. But the young woman's wisdom had been only lightly
tested. Her smooth young face had no lines etched around her eyes
or mouth to give evidence of the joys and sorrows she might have
shared with her sisters. New to the position of leadership, she had
much desire to perform her duties in a way pleasing to the Ministry.
Such colored her listening talents until she seemed to be continually
looking behind every word spoken to her in confession for some
unrevealed sin, instead of merely responding to the admissions of
her sisters' wrongs with kind forgiveness.

Eldress Lilith had come to Harmony Hill from one of the eastern communities. Which one, Sophrena could never remember. Age was such a worrisome thing, not only stealing a person's peace but also impairing her ability to easily recall those things she knew she'd been told. Heaven forbid that she would get like poor Sister Alice who could not be trusted to find her way from her retiring room to the dining table without the aid of another sister. Then again, dear Sister Alice never seemed worried, so perhaps it would not be so ill to become like her. Happy in her place. Happy with her sisters. Of little concern to those in the Ministry.

Sophrena shifted in her chair and was thankful the seat was well woven so that it didn't complain under her weight to give away her uneasiness. She did not like thinking of the Ministry discussing poor Sister Sophrena's lack of unity and peace. True or not. She wanted to squirm in her chair again when she thought of all the times she herself had been concerned about the reluctant spirit of this or that young sister in her charge.

But she had not completely lost all discipline and managed to sit straight in the chair and meet Eldress Lilith's eyes. After all, she had been a proper Shaker for many years, and being a Shaker required a great deal of disciplined behavior. She leaned on that discipline as she waited for whatever else the eldress was going to say.

The younger woman let the silence wrap around them for a long moment. Then she made a clicking noise with her tongue, a habit she had that signaled her effort to remain patient when the proper peace of the household was in question. "Have you nothing to say, my sister?"

Sophrena didn't know what the eldress wanted to hear. Hadn't she already confessed her weariness and the contrary thoughts she'd had regarding Sister Edna? She searched her mind for more sins to confess, but how could she confess what was only an aching feeling inside her that had no words? Another click of Eldress Lilith's tongue poked Sophrena. She would have to say something. It was expected.

"I regret giving the Ministry concern. I realize their time would be better spent praying for our village and the direction of Mother Ann rather than in consideration of my shortcomings." Sophrena dropped her eyes to the table. Perhaps she should confess her reluctance to confess to one so much younger than herself. But age did not matter. Spirit was what mattered. And Sophrena's spirit was as dry and brittle as last year's cornstalks.

"Nay, Sister Sophrena. It is the Ministry's dearest duty to encourage those walking this path of love and salvation. Each sister or brother here is very important to our family. After all, as our Mother Ann teaches, man is more precious than anything he makes, and the best product of industry is character."

"Yea," Sophrena murmured without looking up at the eldress. "I have always endeavored to have good character."

"So you have, my sister. So you have. You are much loved here. That is the reason for the concern over the evident weariness of your spirit." She unwrapped her hands and tapped her fingers on the table a few seconds before once again clicking her tongue. "And for your growing interest in things and people of the world."

"Nay, I have no desire for things of the world." Sophrena pushed the words out too quickly, as though she needed the denial in her own ears even more than in Eldress Lilith's.

"Nor for its people?" The eldress didn't wait for Sophrena to answer. "What of these letters from your worldly family that have brought you tears?"

"Hard times have hit that family and I merely continued to write to them in hopes of offering them some peace."

"One cannot offer what one does not have." There was no click of the tongue this time, only words that Sophrena could not deny.

"Yea, that is true, Eldress. I confess that I have not the proper peace."

The woman reached across the small table between them and touched Sophrena's arm. She studied her a moment before she asked, "What is it you want, Sister Sophrena?"

"What we all want. The gift of a simple spirit. A spirit that does not poke me with unneeded worries."

"A Believer has no reason for worries. Not if we put our trust in the Lord and wait for our Mother Ann's help and guidance."

"Yea. I surely misspoke." Sophrena could not argue with Eldress Lilith's words. She had often said much the same thing to the young novitiates she had guided along the Shaker path over the years. Many had strayed from that path. A few had embraced the peace of a proper Believer and happily continued to give their hands to work for the common good of the Society.

She looked at her own hands with fingers calloused from the peeling knife and stained from working with the apples. She was relieved when the eldress dismissed her to return to her duties.

What is it that you want? Eldress Lilith's question echoed in her head all through the morning as Sophrena worked through the bushels of apples. She wasn't alone in the work. She and Sister Evelyn traded times turning the handle of the peeler or placing the apples on the spindle. Two other sisters worked beside them with another peeler to get the many apples ready for other sisters to cook into applesauce or apple butter. It was a good duty, one that profited the Society in sales or enjoyment at their eating tables, but the task took little thought.

Sophrena would have rather been in the Sisters' workshop making cloth. She had great patience in threading the looms, a tedious process of many days for the larger looms and one that took much concentrated attention since one did not want to tie a thread out of its proper place.

That's what she was, she decided. She set another apple on the spike and watched the blade strip off the peeling when Sister Evelyn turned the handle. Out of her proper place. Peeled of the comfort of her simple beliefs and no longer able to feel the unifying peace in her heart. But why?

Perhaps that question was more to be answered than the question of what she wanted. She had told Eldress Lilith she wanted peace, but was that true? For over twenty-five years she had embraced peace and lived happily in the village. When she thought of it rationally, she saw no reason reaching a milestone of half a century in age should make any difference in that. But she was no longer thinking rationally or simply. Instead she was thinking of Susan's family and how they must be suffering after her death.

She did so wish she could send a gift to the young daughter who of necessity was now caring for the family. Perhaps a silk scarf. She would gladly send her own scarf made from silk produced from the villages' silkworms, but such would not be allowed without permission. She had little trouble imagining Eldress Lilith's frown if she made such a request.

But weren't Believers instructed by Mother Ann to share their plenty with the poor in their neighborhood? Especially with Christmas coming.

Sophrena let a sigh whisper from her as she bent to gather up more apples from the basket. When had she ever thought so much about Christmas? Surely not since she was a child and found a rag doll on her pillow one Christmas morn.

A smile awoke in Sophrena's heart as she remembered the doll's embroidered mouth and eyes and the mere tacking of threads for a nose. She'd carried that doll with her everywhere she went for years. Visible proof of her mother's love that was never spoken aloud.

Life hadn't been easy for her mother, who stared out at each new day with a dark weariness that did not change with the seasons or the chores. Some days Sophrena and her mother worked side by side in the kitchen for hours without a word passing between them.

Good practice for her life with the Shakers, Sophrena thought now as she continued loading the apples on the peeler. Unnecessary conversation was discouraged and silence the friend of spiritual peace and dedicated labor. A worker's mind should be on her tasks. She pulled the slicer down to divide the apple into crisp chunks. As she watched them fall into the catching bucket, the wayward thought crossed her mind to pick up a slice and eat it. What would Sister

Evelyn think if she did that? Sophrena shook her head a little and gathered up six more apples for the spike. Had she lost all discipline? And why did tears keep prickling her eyes over the smallest things?

Her mother had cried. Tears streamed unchecked down her mother's face when Jerome announced he was joining the Shakers and that Sophrena as his wife would have to go with him. Sophrena hadn't cried even though she had no desire to leave her family and join the Shakers. At the same time, she thought anything might be better than the life she was leading married to Jerome.

It had been better.

Her new sisters embraced her and loved her. She fit in the Shaker dresses. She felt in place. The songs in meeting awakened her spirit and her feet were eager to dance. That had surprised her, but the dance had released something within her, freed her to worship. Her unhappy marriage passed out of her memory. She was no longer the Sophrena of the world. She was Sister Sophrena ready to give her heart to God and her hands to work.

She was still ready to do the same. Wasn't she working every day with willing hands? But the Shaker dress no longer fit with comfort. The dark weariness that had weighted down her mother in the world seemed to hover over Sophrena's shoulders now. Life was sliding past her and the rushing days had somehow stolen her contentment. She should stomp and tell the devil to get behind her. That's what Eldress Lilith would tell her to do. That was what Sister Edna would point at her and tell her she had not done.

Another sigh worked up through her. Maybe she needed to ask Brother Kenton for a tonic. Some lemon balm for hysteria. Her heart began beating faster as she imagined Brother Kenton's face listening to her symptoms and then his hands as he prepared the tonic. Oh dear heavens, where was this shivery feeling coming from at the thought of a brother's hands?

She could tell herself she did not know, but it would only be pretense. Ever since spring when she had sprained her ankle and the doctor's strong, slender fingers had moved across her leg to determine the extent of her injury, she had been unable to forget his touch on her skin. She should twirl and shake to rid herself of such wrong thoughts, but instead she stood still and shut her eyes to better experience the feeling.

"What is wrong with you, Sister Sophrena?" Sister Evelyn spoke up from her stool by the apple peeler. "The spindle has been without an apple for a long minute."

"Yea, forgive me, Sister." Sophrena grabbed an apple and in her haste, set it on the spike at a crook. She kept her eyes away from her sister's face as she pulled the apple off and reset it properly. Her hands trembled as she reached for the next apple.

Sister Evelyn turned the wheel at exactly the right speed to take the peeling efficiently from the apple. She watched as Sophrena set another apple in place. "If you feel ill, perhaps you should ask Eldress Lilith's permission to rest in your room this afternoon or even see Brother Kenton for some sort of tonic."

"Nay," Sophrena said. "I am fine. I will do my duty."

"To properly do so you must take care of your body and mind. Mother Ann tells us it takes a whole woman to be a Shaker sister."

"I have been a Believer for many years." Sophrena could not completely keep the irritation out of her voice. Yet another sin of lack of patience she would have need to confess. But would she dare confess the shivery feeling thoughts of Brother Kenton had sent through her? At her age, the very thought of such a sin was ridiculous. She was not a young person who had to stomp out such desires. She long ago picked up her cross of self-denial and carried it faithfully.

She would turn her mind once more to the coming Sacrifice Day to ready herself for the celebration of Christmas. She stepped back into a rhythm with the apples as she pushed aside her wayward thoughts and instead concentrated on the good things the Shaker sisters would cook with the apples for their Christmas dinner. Applesauce cakes. Spiced applesauce to go with the baked ham. Bread fresh from the oven.

But first would be a special meeting with songs and dances to recognize the birth of the Christ. This year Christmas fell on Sunday, so the meeting would be doubly good. A day to rest and pray for the peace promised by the angels on that long ago Christmas.

Peace. That wasn't only what she needed, but what the country needed as well. While their village had weathered the conflict so far, Sophrena couldn't forget the sound of cannons or the reports of casualties. How could she feel peace with the echo of death in her ears? Eldress Lilith could not understand why such thoughts were assaulting Sophrena. Nor could Sophrena.

"Sacrifice Day, a day of atonement, is upon us," the eldress had told Sophrena that morning during her time of confession. "Perhaps you are harboring ill will toward one of your sisters that is upsetting your spirit." She had waved off Sophrena when she tried to speak. "Whatever it is, you will have the opportunity to rid your heart of wrong thinking so you can properly celebrate the gift of the Christ child on Christmas Day."

Sacrifice Day. On that day, she would have much to consider as she begged the Lord to free her from her conflicted spirit. She would wipe from her mind any thought of Brother Kenton's gentle hands. She would fervently pray to feel her proper age and not be tempted by sins of the flesh. She had no reason to dwell on this discontent that kept poking her with wonderings of what she might have missed by putting on the Shaker dress and bonnet.

She had not missed out on love. She had that in plenty from her sisters and brothers here in the village. And from the Lord. She knew his great love in her heart. But there were other kinds of love she had vowed to forget. Family love as the world knew it. That was the loss that was nipping at her heart. She would never know the love of a man and woman. It mattered not that she had been married before she came to the Shaker village. They had known no love. She would never hold a child born of her own body close to her heart and be the one to whisper his name into his ear.

Were those desires so wrong? She had once thought so, but

then Jessamine had shown her the joy of such love. Perhaps loving Jessamine as she imagined a mother would love had given birth to the discontent that had wormed its way into her mind and was eating away her peace.

Sacrifice Day could not come too soon. Confession and concentrated prayers would help her get back in step with her sisters.

The ringing of the bell to signal the midday meal was welcome. She lined up with her sisters and silently found her place at the table. She knelt with them for the silent prayer and then stood and sat at the same instant. The unity of movement was easy for her after so many years. In time, the unity of thought would return as well.

Eldress Lilith stopped her as she left the eating room to start back down the stairs to her duty with the apples. "Sister Willa will be working with Sister Evelyn this afternoon."

Thinking Sister Evelyn had reported her trembling hands, Sophrena said, "I am not ill. I will be able to continue my duty."

"This has naught to do with how you feel." The eldress made the clicking noise with her tongue as furrows formed between her eyebrows. "You have a visitor at the Trustees' House."

"A visitor?" No one had ever come to see her. Her first thought was of Jessamine, but that dear girl was all the way across the country in California.

"No reason to spend words discussing what we cannot know. The Ministry sent for you to greet whoever is there." Eldress Lilith's voice was firm. "Obedience is a trait to be desired."

"Yea." Sophrena bent her head before she turned from the eldress and went out the door.

A visitor for her. From the world. Who could it be? She shoved her hands under her apron to hide their trembling. She knew not why they trembled. She was not afraid, but there was the feeling of something about to happen. A new spirit coming to life within her.

10

"Come in, my sister. You look to be in need of a respite." The woman greeted Heather kindly as she ushered her into the building. "I'm Sister Muriel."

The woman barely gave Heather time to say her name before she turned to lead her past a set of spiral stairways that appeared to almost float upward over Heather's head. When Heather looked up at them, she had to grasp the nearest stair rail to fight off the sudden light-headedness.

"Nay." The woman gently but firmly moved Heather's hand away from the railing. "That is the stairs for the brethren. It is not for us. The sisters must use those on the other side."

"Are we going upstairs?" Heather dropped her hand to her side and willed away her dizziness as she looked toward the winding stairs on the other side of the hallway. Oh, to be able to drop down on that bottom step and find a moment of rest. She was so tired. She had walked across entire states and scrubbed hundreds of uniforms and never felt so weary.

"Nay. Come, follow me and we will see to your needs." She started on down the hallway.

Heather spoke to the woman's back. "I've come to see my aunt, Sophrena." She hesitated. Her mother's letter had given no surname. She knew her aunt had been married, but if she had ever been told her name, it had long been lost in her memory. But surely there could not be that many Sophrenas. "Her maiden name was Prescott." She did know that much.

Sister Muriel's step slowed for a pace at the name, but she didn't stop. "It would be best to save your words until I fetch Eldress Corrine. That way effort will not be wasted speaking them twice over."

Heather said no more as she followed her and let the silence settle around them. Even the woman's footsteps made no noise on the wooden floors, as though she were walking in stocking feet instead of the black shoes that peeked out below her gray dress. Gray like the Rebels. The Rebels who might be shooting at Gideon. Heather pulled in a breath and pushed that thought away as the woman opened a door and motioned her to enter ahead of her.

Heather stepped into the small room and let the warmth from the odd-looking black iron stove wrap around her. A narrow stovepipe shot up from the stove to the tall ceiling. A writing desk was against one of the walls, but strangely enough no chair sat in front of it. Instead three chairs were hung upside down on pegs on a blue railing that ran around the room. The pegs also held a candle sconce and a broom. A rag rug gave the room its only color other than the blue railing. Sister Muriel lifted one of the chairs down from the pegs and set it near the stove.

"Rest here." She motioned Heather toward the chair. "I will return with Eldress Corinne and some refreshment."

Before Heather could lower herself into the chair, the woman was out the door without a sound. Heather sat very still and wondered if her ears had ever been assaulted with such silence. The night before in her father's barn had been dark and lonely, but there was noise. The pigs snuffling in their pen. The hens shifting on their roosts up in the hayloft. Mice scurrying along the timbers of the barn. The screech of an owl from the woods.

Here the silence was so profound she had to push away the thought of being entombed in this small room. She pulled in a steadying breath to stop her head from spinning again. A tomb would have no window, and this room had a tall window to let in plenty of light. Besides, she was not alone in this huge building. Sister Muriel had gone to fetch someone to talk to her. She had simply forgotten how to listen for the quiet sounds of life after becoming accustomed to the crashing sounds of an army.

Heather held her breath and listened intently. Was that the whisper of a step on the floor above her head? A door opened and shut somewhere in the building. She peered out the window again but heard no sound from outside. The window sat back in a pocket that indicated the walls of the building were of double thickness. To hold in warmth.

The warmth was good. So very good. She scooted around in the chair so her feet would be closer to the stove. What did it matter what else was happening in the building? She had a fire to chase away the chill of her ride to the village. She would not worry about what the next hour might bring. She would simply sit in the ladder-back chair that was more comfortable than it looked and be glad of a warm place to wait. Even if Sister Muriel did forget about her there, someone would eventually come to feed the stove more wood.

If she'd learned nothing else while with the army, she'd learned there were many things she couldn't speed up or slow down. The water in her wash pots took a long while to heat even when she had plentiful wood to feed the fire. Night came to the battlefields at its own pace no matter how desperately she prayed for darkness to hurry to end the fighting at least until daylight returned. The night before as an outcast in her father's barn she had wanted the sun to hurry over the horizon. But she could make none of that happen.

Nor could she make anything happen here. She could only wait to see what these strange people would decide to do with her. If they didn't allow it, she might not even see this aunt her mother had hoped would be God's plan for Heather.

Aunt Sophrena. She tried to imagine what she would look like. She had to be getting old. But then her mother had talked of playing with her as a child, that Sophrena had been much younger than Heather's grandfather. Her mother was twenty-one when Heather was born. That meant she was forty-two when she died. This aunt Sophrena might not be so very much older than that. Many officers in the army claimed forty years, even fifty, and led their men into battle with vigor.

Why did her every thought circle back around to battles? But what else could occupy her mind with Gideon marching on with the army? She shut her eyes. She wouldn't think of him fighting the Rebels. Instead she would think about the way he looked as he held her that last morning with the gentle light of love in his eyes. With that thought warming her heart while the fire warmed her body, she let her mind drift back to the first time she saw him at his cousins' house making sorghum.

He had looked so different from the boys she'd known all her life as he led the horse around in a circle to keep the rollers squeezing the juice out of cane his uncle fed into the mill. His red hair lopped down over his forehead and his freckles were bright in the sunshine. She'd never seen anyone with that many freckles. When Gideon spotted her standing there holding onto Lucas to keep him out of trouble, he had grinned and grabbed up the boy to perch him on the broad back of the workhorse.

"Grab a couple of handfuls of the old girl's mane there, kid," he told Lucas with a a big grin over at Heather. "We wouldn't want you falling off and cracking open your head before you have a chance to introduce me to your sister. She is your sister and not your girl, isn't she?"

Lucas had laughed, excited to be on the horse, even if it was only a tired old workhorse. Heather had smiled a bit at Gideon, but that was all. She hadn't encouraged his attentions that day. He was too different. He even sounded different with a northern twang to his voice. Simon said he was from up in Ohio and that he wouldn't be around that long.

"Joey says he don't know why he decided to come visit them, unless he thought he could find some freckle-removing juice down this way," Simon said. "He's needing it for certain."

All the boys made fun of his freckles, but Gideon just laughed right along with them until they began to see past his freckles. And he didn't head back north. At least not right away. Instead he headed over to Heather's house. At first he pretended it was to see Simon, but it wasn't very many days until everybody knew he was courting Heather. He took Lucas and Willie fishing but told Heather she'd better come along to make sure he didn't lose one of the boys. He did handstands in the yard to make her mother laugh and gave Jimmy rides on his shoulders so he could be taller than his brothers, even Simon.

And Heather tumbled right into the quicksand of love. She sank fast with no interest in being rescued. They shared their first kiss in the golden light of a harvest moon in late October. They were together every moment possible through November. He went home in December.

"But I'll be back next summer," he had promised. On the way home from church, he pulled her off the road in behind Mr. Johnson's barn. Sheltered there from the early winter wind and hidden from curious eyes, he kissed her before he asked, "You'll wait for me, won't you, Heather Lou? You won't let another boy steal your heart if I'm not around to chase him away."

"They can't steal what's not here. You'll be taking my heart home with you," Heather had whispered.

She couldn't stand the thought of him leaving her. She wanted to go with him. She was nearly eighteen. Lots of girls married that young. She would have gone with him in a minute, but he hadn't asked her. He'd kissed her. He'd held her close. He'd even said he loved her, but he hadn't said anything about getting married and loving her forever.

Her mother said that was good. They hadn't really known each other very long. It was better to be patient when a person was talking about love for the rest of her life. She reminded Heather that he'd promised to be back in the spring, and if the feelings were still strong between them, then would be time enough to think about the future.

The future. How easy it had been to dream about the future through the cold months of that winter of 1861. He wrote to her. She wrote him back even though her father frowned on the exchange.

"Plenty of good boys right here in the neighborhood," he told her. "No sense you pining after some boy way up north."

But she hadn't given any other boy the time of day no matter how they sidled up to her at church. Gideon had taken her heart back to Ohio with him, and she was doing no more than marking time until he returned. Then he would ask her to marry him. Then her father would see Gideon's good points. Then they could find a little place and settle down to begin the rest of their lives.

She didn't pay much attention to what was going on in the world. It didn't have all that much to do with her back on the ridge where they lived. At least that's what she thought until April when the Rebels fired on Fort Sumter and tore the country apart. The North on one side and the South on the other, with Kentucky right in the middle, leaning first one way, then another. Neighbors became enemies. Families split, with brothers lining up in opposing armies ready to shoot at one another. Gideon stayed in Ohio—a Northerner through and through.

After Simon shouldered his hunting gun and headed south, Heather's father threw Gideon's letters in the fire when they came. Yankees were the enemy, and he forbade Heather to persist in imagining herself to be in love with one of them.

But she had persisted. Oh, how she had persisted. Nothing could keep her from loving Gideon then or now. She shifted in the chair by the Shakers' stove to ease her aching back as she cradled the baby growing inside her. Sweet evidence of her persistence.

"Little one, we will see your father again. We will." She spoke the words aloud for she needed them for her own ears, and even though she kept her voice very soft, it seemed too loud in the silence of the Shaker house.

As if her spoken words had drawn them, Sister Muriel and another woman came into the room. Sister Muriel carried a tray that Heather tried not to eye too eagerly. She moistened her dry lips and looked away from the steaming cup and bowl on the tray to the woman who had come in with Sister Muriel. She wore the same type dress with the overlapping white collar and the same bonnet covering her hair, but she was much older and even sterner looking than Sister Muriel.

Heather pushed up out of her chair to meet the women. She didn't know if she should smile or try to look as serious as they did. Perhaps smiling was against their rules here.

Sister Muriel stepped back from the tray without speaking. She tucked her hands under her apron and lowered her eyes. The older woman motioned toward the tray and spoke in a voice that had a quiver in it. Heather wasn't sure if that was due to her age or perhaps from infrequent use in this silent place.

"Please, bring your chair over and eat," the woman said. "It appears you have double need of sustenance."

Heather didn't hesitate to do as she was told. She was hungry. The breakfast Willie had brought her that morning was no more than a faint memory. She did bend her head and silently thank the Lord for his provisions before she picked up the cup. She had expected coffee or tea, but it was warm, spiced cider. She tried not to guzzle it, but she didn't know when last she'd had anything so delicious. She tasted the apples as the warm liquid slid down her throat. When she spooned up bites of the vegetable soup, it was even better. With each bite, she could feel her energy reviving.

"Thank you so much," she said between bites. A frown flitted across the older woman's face as behind her Sister Muriel gave a slight shake of her head in warning. Heather wasn't sure why, but she decided not to chance any more wrong words. She'd concentrate on the soup and wait for whatever they had to say.

The spoon clanging against the bowl sounded loud in the total silence, but she did manage not to slurp the soup. She ate every bite and would have licked the bowl if the two women hadn't been watching her so closely. She laid down her spoon and started to stand again, but the older woman put a hand on her shoulder.

"Nay, don't get up, my child. You look very tired." Her lips made a slight curve up into a smile. "I'm Eldress Corrine. Sister Muriel says you have asked to see one of our other sisters, Sister Sophrena."

"She's my aunt. Well, great aunt," Heather said.

"In the world perhaps. Here we don't recognize such titles. We are all brothers and sisters one with another," the eldress said.

The soup she'd just eaten shifted uneasily in her stomach. In spite of the woman telling her not to, she stood up to better plead her cause. "But I have to see her. My mother told me to."

"Your mother?" Eldress Corinne said.

"Yes. She died a few months ago." Heather's hand went to her pocket to touch her mother's letter.

"The ways of the world are hard. Where is the father of your child?" the woman asked. Sister Muriel raised her head a little, as though interested in Heather's answer too.

"The army."

"Which one?" the eldress asked.

"Does it matter?" Heather peered at the woman and wondered if that was a proper answer.

"Nay, we are against all war, but have compassion on the soldiers caught up in the sinful conflict." The expression on Eldress Corrine's face didn't change. She stared at Heather with eyes calm as a still pool. "And so, do you have no home, my child?"

"I have nothing but what I hold in my hands," Heather said.

"How true of us all." The eldress did smile at her then. She reached over and touched Heather's arm. "Worry not, my sister. We will not turn you away."

"And will I be allowed to see my aunt?"

"Yea, she has been sent for. I think I hear her coming now."

Heather had heard nothing, but the elder woman's ears must have been more attuned to the silence. The door was opening and another woman, again in the same type dress, was coming into the room. She brought with her the fresh scent of apples and the outdoors.

Heather stared at her and grabbed the back of the chair as her head began to spin once more. This woman was looking straight at Heather with her mother's eyes. Eyes she had so wanted to see and that now were peering out of a stranger's face.

11

A young sister was waiting in the front hall of the Trustee House to point Sophrena to the room where her visitor waited. Sister Hilda trailed along behind Sophrena, obviously as curious about who might be asking for Sophrena as Sophrena was. A hundred wonderings had crossed through her mind on the short walk from the Centre Family House to the building where all business with the outside world was conducted.

She had guided numerous young sisters along the Shaker way over the years. One of those who had left the village to try worldly living might be seeking a return to the Society. Such was not uncommon since the world sometimes proved less than welcoming. If so, she would do her best to hide her own discontent, for there was much good in living the Shaker life. Much good.

Life in the world could hold many sorrows. She'd known some of her own and had heard many others from novitiates. The Shaker village offered peace while those of the world were beset by war and hardship. She knew such was true. She had always eagerly gathered the fruits of Shaker peace and been nourished by them. Never before had the worms of worldly thinking spoiled their goodness.

Sophrena pushed all that aside. Wondering and guessing served no purpose. Whoever had come asking for her would soon stand in front of her and then all questions would be answered.

Sister Muriel opened the door for Sophrena and stepped aside to allow her to enter the room before she took Sister Hilda's arm and walked her back out into the hallway. She shut the door quietly but firmly behind them, leaving Sophrena alone with Eldress Corinne and the visitor. The tattered edges of a much worn, soiled brown skirt peeked out behind the eldress to give evidence the visitor was someone in need. In spite of the curiosity springing to life inside her, Sophrena did not try to peer around the eldress. When she was ready for Sophrena to see the visitor, she would move. It would not be proper for Sophrena to try to hurry her.

Eldress Corinne had come to Harmony Hill from one of the eastern villages and possessed a tranquil air that nothing ruffled. Through storms, strangers from the world appearing on their doorsteps, even Confederate guerilla forces riding through their village demanding food, she stayed calm, sure of her Shaker walk. As sure as Sophrena had been in years past.

"Someone has asked to see you, Sister Sophrena." She moved aside to allow Sophrena a clear view of the young woman whose eyes popped open too wide at the sight of Sophrena. Eyes the very same hazel mix of gray, blue, and green as Sophrena's own.

Sophrena knew her at once. She was that much like her mother. The very image of Susan who had been not much younger than this woman when Sophrena last saw her. Unmarried as yet and so not heavy with child as this girl was.

This had to be Heather, the daughter Susan had been so worried about, the one who had married a Union soldier against her father's wishes. Sophrena had prayed for the girl so often in the past year that she had begun to feel as if she did know her. Now here she was standing right in front of her as if those prayers had summoned her.

The color drained from the girl's face, and she let out a startled gasp. She threw out her hand as though reaching for something to grasp.

"She's going to swoon." Without ceremony, Sophrena pushed past Eldress Corinne to grab the girl before she fell. The eldress scooted the chair under the young woman, and Sophrena lowered her carefully into it. "Are you all right, Heather?"

The girl nodded, but she continued to lean heavily against Sophrena as she pulled in her breath too rapidly. Eldress Corinne leaned down to speak directly into her face. "Breathe slowly, child. In and out. Slowly. If you keep trying to grab all the air at once, you will only make yourself more apt to swoon."

"I'm sorry. I'm not usually prone to swooning." The girl's voice was not much above a whisper.

"Perhaps it is your condition," the eldress said kindly. "Is it near your time?"

"No, not for weeks," Heather said.

"Babies have been known to come before their proper time," Eldress Corinne said. "It could be we should send for our doctor here. Brother Kenton."

Sophrena tried to concentrate on the girl leaning against her and not think about how just the mention of Brother Kenton's name made her heart lurch inside her chest. A woman her age should not entertain such thoughts. A faithful, proper Believer would not be tempted by the sound of a brother's name.

"I am having none of the sorts of pains I remember my mother having with my little brothers." The girl's voice grew stronger. "I think it's only that I am so tired and . . ." Her voice trailed off as she straightened in the chair to look from the eldress to Sophrena.

"And what, child?" the eldress asked with an edge of sternness. "If we are to help you, you must be forthcoming with the truth and not slip sideways into stuttering evasions."

The young woman placed a protective hand on her mounded middle, shut her eyes, and pulled in a deep breath. When she opened them, she again looked up at Sophrena instead of the

eldress as she spoke. "I have been with the army since the summer of '62."

"A camp follower." Eldress Corinne stated the words without
emotion, but her disapproval was evident.

"You could say that. I was a laundress with my husband's unit.
A washerwoman. Hard but honorable work."

"And necessary work," Sophrena added.

The eldress leveled her eyes at Sophrena. "Perhaps we should
hear our visitor out before we add words to her talk."

"Yea." Sophrena bent her head and studied the wide plank floor-
ing. It was beginning to amaze her how many times she could
disregard the discipline of years. The eldress would let her know
when it was proper to speak.

Heather, whether sensing Sophrena's unease or simply needing
encouragement herself, reached over to grasp Sophrena's hand as
she continued her story. "I was fortunate to get the job as laundress
since it did allow my husband to be with me when no battle was
going on."

"That appears quite evident," Eldress Corinne said. "As you
are with child."

Heather must have noted the censure in the woman's voice because she lowered her head. Sophrena bit the inside of her lip to
keep from speaking. Instead she tightened her grip on the girl's
fingers as silence pressed in on them.

"That I am," she said finally in soft words. "A blessing, but
Gideon thought it best if I came home since the army was moving
south to engage the enemy. So I made my way home only to find
my mother passed on and my father unwelcoming."

"Such are the sorrows of the world where the conflicts of war and
family bring nothing but unhappiness." Eldress Corinne straightened up and studied Heather for a long moment before she went
on. "And so, have you come to us seeking salvation and peace on
this day?"

Heather lifted her head and looked straight at the eldress. "I came seeking my aunt. Sophrena. My mother held back the grave to guide me here and then . . ." Her voice faded and tears began to slide down her cheeks. She pulled in a steadying breath and looked up at Sophrena as if Eldress Corinne was forgotten. "And then when I did see you, it was as though my mother had come back to life. You are so like her."

"Many took us for sisters when we were young," Sophrena said.

"Now you have many sisters," Eldress Corinne reminded her as she took control of the conversation again. She peered down at Heather with rekindled kindness. "You can be one of our sisters, my child."

Heather's shoulders tightened. "I will not give up my baby." She lifted her chin and stared at the eldress. "I have heard you do not allow families or a woman to mother her own child."

"My dear girl, we are all of one family. Brothers and sisters with the Christ and our Mother Ann. Many years ago the Lord revealed to our Mother Ann that the small individual family of which you speak causes nothing but heartache and troubles. Here we love all the same as it will be in heaven. As it was meant to be here before sin came into the world. We shut out that sin, and all sin, from our villages and know love as the Eternal Father intended us to love."

"The love I have for my child is not a sin." Heather pulled her hand away from Sophrena to cradle her abdomen. "Does not the Bible teach us that a man should leave his mother and father and cleave to his wife?"

Eldress Corinne's smile was genuine. "Yea, there is such a passage, but that's in the sinful world. Here at Harmony Hill we have brought heaven down to us and thus must live by heavenly rules instead of worldly ones."

"I cannot believe it right to separate a mother from her child even in heaven. Not if God is love as the Bible says."

"You cling to the baser thoughts of love, my child, and not of the love that flows down to us from Mother Ann." The eldress reached her hands toward heaven. "The Spirit gifts us with much love. Isn't that right, Sister Sophrena?"

"Yea, we have love in abundance." Sophrena answered as the eldress expected her to answer, but then she added, "Even so, it sometimes takes time for those from the world to understand our ways."

"I will never give up my child." Heather's face was set and determined. And very weary. "As Mary held and loved the baby Jesus on that first Christmas so long ago, I will hold and love my baby. Even if I have to do so in a stable as she did."

Again Sophrena held her tongue. She wanted to put her arms around the girl and promise her everything would be fine. She wanted to tell her she would take care of her, but it would do little good to promise what she could not give. She had no home other than her bed in the retiring room. A room she shared with five other sisters. She did not even have a stable to offer her.

"You knew of our ways and yet you still came to us," Eldress Corinne said.

"I did." Heather stared down at her hands protecting the baby inside her. "But I had also heard you were very kind and so I hoped. My father beat down the hope I had of home, but my mother's written words gave me hope that I might find help here with my aunt."

Sophrena let a silent prayer wing from her mind straight toward heaven that a way might be found to keep the girl's hopes alive. Winter was coming. They couldn't turn the poor child away. Not in her condition. Hadn't Mother Ann always instructed her followers to show much charity to the poor? And especially so at Christmastime?

She glanced over at the eldress and wondered if she dared say as much aloud. Eldress Corinne was much more compassionate than Eldress Lilith, but at the same time, she would not expect Sophrena to doubt her ability to capably handle a problem such as Heather and her condition. She would frown on the way Sophrena's heart was reaching out to Heather in a way that lacked the Believer's discipline and instead went back to the years before she came to the Shaker village. All the way back to Susan as a bright-eyed child running after Sophrena, begging for one more piggyback ride. Oh, if only Sophrena could pick up this child in front of her and somehow carry her to safety. But she had nothing to offer her except heartfelt prayers sent heavenward.

The eldress too stood in an attitude of prayer for a long moment. When at last she lifted her head, she said, "Yea, it is our duty to be kind. A way will be found to help you, my young sister. That too is our duty. We don't turn away those in need whatever their spiritual lackings. Instead we keep those shortcomings in our prayers."

Sophrena sent up another silent prayer of thanksgiving for Eldress Corinne. Then she dared speak the idea that had come to her while the eldress prayed. "There is the cabin where the Jeffersons stayed while Brother Omer attempted to get his wife of the world to agree to the Shaker life."

"Yea, he will be rewarded for his faithfulness while she will suffer for her foolishness of running back to the sinful world."

"If the Ministry allows, my young relative from the world could stay in the cabin."

Eldress Corinne eyed Heather. "She doesn't look able to care for herself. There would be fire to maintain in that cabin and water to be carried."

"I could do that," Heather spoke up. "My years as washerwoman have made me strong."

"So you say." Doubt was evident in Eldress Corrine's voice.

"Nay, she is too close to her time to stay alone." Sophrena spoke up quickly. "If the Ministry agrees, I could stay with her until the baby is born or until her husband or her father comes for her."

"Father will not come," Heather said without a shred of doubt. Then her voice got louder, seeming to be trying to push the same conviction into her next words. "But Gideon will. When the war is over. And it will be over soon."

"Those in the world will always be warring over something,

but such is not our concern at this moment." The eldress looked from Heather to Sophrena. "Are you sure, Sister Sophrena, that such a living arrangement for even a few weeks will not reek of too much worldliness?"

"I have lived as a Believer for many years. A few weeks will not change what I believe is truth." The words were the right words, but inside Sophrena, doubts were poking her. Not new ones that had just sprung to life at the thought of being away from her sisters, but the same doubts that had been poking her for months. It would be best if Eldress Corinne did not note those poking doubts.

"Yea, that is so." Eldress Corinne bent her head a little in acceptance. "Let me consult the Ministry. They may be able to devise a better way."

Heather didn't speak until the eldress went out, leaving them alone. "The Ministry? Is that like your preacher?"

"Not exactly," Sophrena said. "We have two elders and two eldresses who have been chosen by the spirit to lead our village. Their decision will be fair and wise."

"Will they let me stay at this cabin you mentioned?"

"Yea, I think they will."

"With you to help me?"

Sophrena touched the girl's shoulder. "My heart is praying it so."

The girl reached up and covered Sophrena's hand. "I am sorry to be bringing you trouble and upsetting your life."

"Nay, worry not. It is God's plan."

12

God's plan. The words kept running through Heather's head. Written by her mother. Spoken by her aunt.

Her aunt was silent now as she led the way along the walkways through the village. She did look back with concern toward Heather and slowed her pace until a turtle could have stayed abreast of them.

That was fine with Heather. The last few days had drained her energy until every step forward was an exercise of will. When it was determined that the plan proposed by her aunt was acceptable to their leaders, the eldress had suggested a chair with wheels for her aunt to push her to the cabin they proposed to be her sanctuary. With her aunt as her caretaker. But Heather had assured the woman she could walk.

She was walking. She had faced many things more trying than this walk through the Shaker village. The Lord would give her strength. Hadn't he already supplied this plan? Not only supplied it, but planted it in her mother's mind and the mind of this woman who looked so like her mother. Heather had not expected that. A gift and a sorrow at the same time to see her mother's eyes watching her with curious kindness from this stranger's face.

Not a stranger. Your aunt. Family. Her mother's voice whispered inside her mind as if she were walking along beside Heather. Hadn't she promised she would always be with Heather? No matter what happened.

After the large buildings they had passed, the cabin looked very small nestled there on the edge of the village. But smoke was curling up out of the chimney. A man was carrying wood up the steps into the cabin. Her aunt stopped walking and put her hand on Heather's arm.

"We will wait here until Brother Henry has finished supplying us with wood. It would not be proper to disturb his work. But it is good the elders sent him ahead of us so there will be warmth inside for you."

"Is there an outhouse?" Calls of nature had been a constant problem during her time with the army, especially after she was in the family way. Heather looked around, hoping the privy would not be too distant.

"Yea, the sisters' privy at the Gathering House is not far. Come, I'll show you."

The outhouse looked to have been recently swept out. Not one cobweb dripped down forgotten from the top corners.

Back at the cabin, Sophrena ushered her inside where the fire burning brightly in the fireplace spoke of home. The two rooms were small with only the barest furnishings. Chairs like those in the house she'd just come from were pushed up to a plain table in the middle of the front room. Shelves on the back wall held a few dishes and round boxes but no books. A cupboard sat in the corner and a sewing rocker was next to the fire. The adjoining room held two narrow beds, a chest, and a washstand. A fire also burned in the bedroom's fireplace. Another rocker sat next to that fire. Candles waited on the mantels ready to hold back the night.

Sophrena ushered Heather to the chair in front of the fire, then looked uncertain, even a bit uneasy. "Or perhaps you should lie down."

Heather wondered if her aunt might already be regretting her offer of help that promised to take her from the life she'd been living.

"I'm fine, Aunt Sophrena," Heather said, even though her head felt heavy on her shoulders and the thought of lying down did sound wonderful. She wouldn't want Sophrena to think she had no manners. Besides, she felt too dirty to lie down on the white covers of the bed she'd glimpsed in the other room. Perhaps she could rest in the chair and then wash before night.

Her nightclothes in her valise were still clean from her last washtubs before she started home.

"Aunt Sophrena," Sophrena echoed her words. "Your mother sometimes called me that when we were girls. She thought it funny that I could be her aunt and only a little older than she. But I never thought to hear anyone call me that after I came to the Shakers." She pulled one of the straight chairs away from the table and scooted it over in front of the fire beside Heather before she sat down. "We are all sisters here."

"Then should I call you Sister Sophrena?"

Sophrena stared at the fire a long moment before she answered, "Yea, that might be best. But it had a sweet sound when you said aunt. A tempting sound."

"Tempting?" Heather frowned over at her, but Sophrena didn't notice. She was still staring into the fire. "I don't understand."

"Nor do I." Her aunt sighed. "Nor do I."

"You won't have to stay with me all the time, Sister Sophrena." Heather hesitated a bit before speaking the name, but she would get used to it. Aunt Sophrena had sat oddly on her tongue as well. She went on. "I am capable of taking care of myself. I am just weary from the trip home and my concerns for my husband."

"I told you to worry not about my time, child. I must do what the Ministry says. It is the way of the Believer to be obedient." She smiled over at Heather. "Besides, this is a gift to me as well as you. It will give me time to consider my walk and clear wrong thoughts from my heart."

Heather looked at the woman staring into the fire again and wondered what wrong thoughts could be bedeviling her. She pushed her curiosity away. Didn't she have enough worries of her own? Gideon. The war. Her father. Her mother's words telling her to be forgiving. But her mother hadn't seen the way he had shut Heather out in the cold when she so needed a place to rest. Or the way he tried to keep her own brothers and sister from greeting her so they had to sneak out into the dark of night. Such a father did not deserve forgiveness.

Sophrena gave herself a bit of a shake and stood up. "It is not a Believer's way to sit when there is work to be done. Not unless it is a time of rest or the Sabbath."

She looked around at the wall before she set the chair back over at the table. "The brothers need to put some pegs in these logs so there would be places to put things out of the way." She sounded almost cross.

Heather thought of the chairs off the floor in the large house. "Why do you hang chairs upside down on the wall?"

Sophrena turned back to Heather. "Upside down, a chair will not collect dust to soil one's clothes when one sits upon it. We hang chairs and other things on the pegs out of the way to make cleaning a room easier. Good spirits won't stay where there is dirt. Mother Ann taught that from the very beginning."

Heather looked down at her dress, soiled from her long trip home. Her hands carried the grime of her travels too and she did not want to even think of how her face and hair might look. It was good she spotted no mirror in this place. "Then I suppose no good spirits will come close to me."

"Such will be remedied before the evening meal." Sophrena touched her shoulder. "Rest here while I fetch bathing water and clean garments for you. We have only dresses like these we wear." Sophrena ran her hand across her skirt.

"I will be grateful for whatever you can spare as long as the waist does not bind me," Heather said.

"Yea, I will choose a dress with that in mind." Sophrena went to the door, but turned back to say, "Eldress Corinne will be sending Brother Kenton to check on you." She looked all around the room without letting her eyes fall on Heather, as though perhaps just speaking of Heather's condition made her uneasy. Then her voice softened. "Brother Kenton will treat you with great kindness."

Her cheeks looked flushed against the white cap she wore over her hair as she opened the door. Perhaps from the fire. Heather put her hand up to her own cheek. It no doubt was red from the warmth of the fire as well.

Sophrena was all business when she returned with a bucket of water in one hand and a bundle of clothes in the other. She filled the kettle to swing over the fire. She made no attempt at conversation and neither did Heather. It seemed silence suited these Shaker people and her aunt was one of them. Besides, the silence was somehow comforting in this small cabin where it had been unnerving in the big house with the eldress eying her. Heather had felt something like a stray cat showing up on the Shaker woman's doorstep. Kindness compelled her to feed the creature, but she had no intention of soiling her hands by offering it the comfort of a stroke down its fur.

But Sophrena appeared eager to reach out to Heather. At the same time, she seemed unsure of exactly how best to help this stray who had shown up out of nowhere to upset her ordered life. Her touches were like that of a butterfly, fluttering and light. Heather thought of stepping closer to her aunt and embracing her, but she too was hesitant. While the woman was undeniably family, she was yet a stranger. It mattered not how much she resembled Heather's mother. That didn't bring Heather's mother back to life. Heather would never feel her mother's arms around her again while on this earth. She had only the memory of her love and the letter in her pocket to guide her.

The woman helped undo Heather's dress and then gathered it up after Heather stepped out of it. Again she seemed uneasy as her eyes dropped to Heather's rounded form under her shift and quickly away before she said, "There are clean undergarments as well."

She started to turn away, but Heather reached out a hand to stop her. "The baby is kicking up quite a fuss. Would you like to feel?"

Without waiting for an answer, she took Sophrena's free hand and placed it on her shift where the baby pushed against her skin. Her aunt's eyes widened, and Heather thought she might jerk her hand away when she released it. But she did not. Instead she closed her eyes and kept her hand solidly on Heather's stomach, as though absorbing the feel of the baby. When she opened her eyes, tears slipped from their corners to slide unnoticed down her cheeks.

She looked at Heather and asked, "How does it feel to carry a new life within you?" She dropped her hand back to her side and waited for Heather's answer.

"At times, uncomfortable." Heather smiled as she put her hand where Sophrena's had been and gently massaged the elbows or knees poking against her. "But uncomfortable or not, it is good. A natural thing. As God intended when love forms a child."

"We do not believe in such love here at Harmony Hill. Or at any of the Shaker villages. We live as brothers and sisters the way Mother Ann decreed was best."

"Why would she decide that?" Heather didn't try to hide her puzzlement. "What kind of world would it be without babies?"

"In a perfect world, the kind of world the Believers hope to have in their villages, babies would be given just as Mary was given the Christ child to bear."

"Is that what you believe, Sister Sophrena?" Heather asked.

"I have doubts that everyone in the world will ever seek the Shaker way of perfect devotion. So I think there will always be babies and children in need of a home. The Believers stand ready to supply that home with hope some of those children might embrace the Shaker way."

"As you have," Heather said.

"As I have." Sophrena did not meet Heather's eyes as she lifted the hem of her apron to dash away the remnants of her tears. "I was not a child when I came to Harmony Hill, but I was in need of the good love the sisters and brothers here offered to me so freely."

"Did you not have a happy marriage?"

"Nay." The word was spoken abruptly. "There is much unhappiness in the world."

"So are you happy now?" Heather spoke the question, even though she could tell Sophrena was anxious to be shed of the talk of marriage and happiness.

"It is a place of peace and love," Sophrena said. "Not the love of the world, but the love of God. Here, we give our hearts to God."

"I love the Lord, but I don't think he puts limits on love here on earth. Love is part of his design."

"Yea, your thoughts of love are worldly ones. Harmony Hill is different and you may understand our ways better after living among us."

"I won't give up my child," Heather said.

"Worry not, my young sister. That would not even be possible for you right now. You are the vessel of life for your baby. Wait to worry about tomorrow when the day comes." Sophrena kept her voice soft and calm. "I will go gather up some necessary supplies and give you the privacy of your bath. Brother Kenton will be here before the evening meal to determine if all is well with you."

"If he is a Shaker, can he know anything about birthing babies?"

"He was a doctor before he came to the Shakers. So I am confident he has helped babies come into the world."

Sophrena turned away from Heather to busily poke at the fire before adding a chunk of wood. She brushed her hands off on her apron as she straightened back up, keeping her eyes from Heather's face. It was clear she was uncomfortable talking about the birth.

"Mother never had anyone with her except a neighbor lady

who helped birth babies. I'm sure I'll be fine with your help, Sister Sophrena."

But would she? She had to wonder about that as Sophrena grabbed up Heather's soiled dress and hurried out without a backward glance. Perhaps Heather was asking too much of a woman who had lived away from the normal ways of families for so long. Heather stared at the door Sophrena had firmly pushed shut behind her. How could these people believe that babies weren't a gift from God? Was not the Christ the greatest gift ever? A baby born and placed in a manger.

Heather let out a long breath. She was here and here she would stay. At least until the baby came. She had little choice unless the war ended before then and Gideon returned for her. That wasn't likely no matter how many prayers she sent up for peace. She shut her eyes and remembered the last embrace they'd shared before he marched away from her. She would see him again. She would. Please, Lord, she would.

13

Gideon's division made the last part of the trip to Nashville by boat down the Cumberland River. Gideon worked his way out to a spot close to the rail on the crowded decks where he could see the water flowing past them. He aimed to be where he could jump into the river if the Confederates surprised them with a cannonball to the broadsides. It didn't matter that he'd never been that good of a swimmer. His swimming would be better than his sinking with the boat.

Jake White laughed at him. "You won't get a chance to swim. You're right out here where the sharpshooters can pick you off."

"No Rebel can shoot that good." Gideon looked toward the riverbank. It wasn't actually all that far away. And some of the Rebels were fair shots when they had time to take aim. Sitting up in the trees along the river, they might have plenty of time to steady their shots. "Leastways they haven't shot good enough to hit me yet," he added without quite as much confidence in his voice.

"We've had the luck of the Irish so far." Jake settled down beside Gideon. The air off the river was cold and Gideon was glad for Jake's broad back blocking some of the wind.

"I'm not Irish," Gideon said.

"I'm Irish enough for the both of us," Jake said. "I'll see to it that you make it home to see that wee little bairn after he's born."

"And how are you going to do that?" Gideon twisted to look Jake in the face.

"Now think straight, lad. If you were a Johnny Reb sharpshooter with only one shell to spend before a boat full of Yankees got out of range, who would you aim for? A smallish target like you or a big one like me?"

"He might want to prove his skill." Gideon studied the riverbank again to see if he could catch the glint of light on a gun barrel.

"True enough," Jake agreed easily. "The Rebels are a strange bunch. That yell of theirs can send chills down a man's back."

Gideon shivered as he pulled his jacket closer around him. He'd heard the Rebel yell, seen the charges, been deafened by the cannons, and so far come out with not so much as a scratch. But a man couldn't be lucky forever when he faced enemy fire. Could be, the coming battle might be his last in spite of what he'd told Heather before they parted.

He smiled, thinking of Heather safe with her family now. Her mother would take care of his Heather Lou and his baby too. He did so want to see that baby. He shut his eyes and imagined the little tyke in Heather's arms. A tiny boy with dark hair like Heather's. He wouldn't wish his red locks and freckles on anybody, even though he was used to them and the jibes they brought. Some things were only funny the first few times a fellow heard them and sometimes not all that funny even then. He'd scraped a lot of knuckles in fistfights before he figured out laughing along with the jokester made for fewer bruises.

But wonder of wonders, Heather hadn't minded his red hair and freckles. From their very first meeting, she was ready to laugh with him instead of at him. They had laughed about all sorts of things that looked fresh and more wonderful staring at them through eyes of love.

He stared down at the water flowing past, taking him farther away from her, and hated how empty his arms felt. Behind him, Jake had leaned back against the railing and was snoring. The man could sleep anywhere. Something Heather had said about him too. A soldier had to take his rest when and where he could. But sleep had come easier with her by his side. Now miles were between them and he could do nothing but remember the sweet blessing of her head on his shoulder and the touch of her hand on his back.

She was his luck, his gift, his blessing, and his love all rolled up together. He pulled his knees up to his chest and dropped his head down on them. She prayed for him. He had watched her kneel in their tent and silently mouth prayers before she lay down beside him. She asked him once if he prayed. She never saw him bending his head in prayer.

He told her, sure, he prayed. It was just that he wasn't good with prayer words. Better to let someone else say the prayers and let him do the fighting. Besides, he'd already gotten the answer to his prayers. His Heather Lou.

But now he had no idea how long it would be until she was in his arms again. He was headed toward a new battle with who knew what results. Then again, she was about to enter a battlefield herself. Women died trying to birth babies.

It was no wonder sleep eluded him.

14

The days passed into December. It was peaceful in the cabin with Heather. It somehow felt right to Sophrena, almost as if she had gone back in time to the years before she came to the Shakers. But then she would remind herself that the years before she came to the Shakers were not peaceful. After her marriage, one miserable day had piled onto another in the small house where she and Jerome had started housekeeping. What she was imagining was only a wish of what might have been.

She still felt unsettled when she thought about the future, and when Brother Kenton came to examine Heather or bring her a new tonic, she felt worse than unsettled. She was the same as those foolish young sisters she had once tried to guide along the peaceful path of obedience to the Believers' rules. Those girls had kept one foot firmly planted in the world, and most had soon let the other foot follow it away from Harmony Hill. They had never wanted to take up their cross and change their thinking.

She had been so sure of the truth then. The Lord had guided her to this village where a new life awaited her. The Lord had blessed her with love here. She rejoiced in picking the fruit of the spirit and living a simple life. Such a life was a gift. She believed that. She wanted none of the trappings of the world. She had no need of fancy dresses or carriages to ride in like women of the world. She desired nothing more than the opportunity to work with her hands and feel the love of God within her heart.

She was content to let others point the way for her. To do as the Ministry ordered. To whirl and dance to show her love of the Lord. To embrace the Believer's way. But then she'd turned fifty. The Believers didn't celebrate the birth dates of their members. It was only another day of no particular importance. Age was of no concern in heaven and so the same was true at Harmony Hill where heaven's rules were heeded and worldly things forgotten.

But while she'd given her birthdays little thought over the years, the number stayed in her mind. How could one forget the number of years one had been blessed with life? But no number had poked at her the way fifty did, worrying her like a thorn from a blackberry vine that worked deep into her finger and couldn't be dug out. Temptations she never dreamed would beset her came and sat on her shoulders. Those confessions of wrong thinking she had heard from the novitiates she had once guided toward spiritual purity must have hidden out inside her and now were surfacing one after another.

A month after her birthday, Brother Kenton Todd had come among them from the Union village in Ohio when Harmony Hill was in need of a doctor. Sister Lettie had passed into heaven and Brother Benjamin had developed painful joints that limited his doctoring ability. He'd returned to the New Lebanon village in the East to spend his days compounding new mixtures of herbs in hopes of finding something to relieve the rheumatism pains suffered by him and many of the older Believers.

Something about the new brother had drawn Sophrena's eyes. Even when she tried most not to notice him, her eyes would seek him out during meeting the way she'd once seen weaker-willed sisters let their gaze be drawn to the brothers' side of the meetinghouse.

She had zealously taken part in the stomping or shaking songs to rid her mind of such wayward thoughts. She thought she had succeeded. The fretful worry of missing something necessary stayed within her, but she kept her eyes where they were meant to look. She had no desire for forbidden fruit. She only wanted to recapture the peace she'd once known that now seemed to be leaking away from her. The new brother was not the cause of her melancholy. She had surely simply carried that seed forward from her mother.

A couple of months after Brother Kenton came to Harmony Hill, he was in attendance at the same union meeting as Sophrena. They gathered with three other sisters and three other brothers in Brother Jackson's room to talk of the events of the week. Such meetings were held each week to allow small groups of brothers and sisters to converse. A row of chairs for the brethren and a row of chairs for the sisters were placed across from one another well apart to avoid any possibility of touching during these times of shared words.

That night, Brother Jackson had talked of the war and how those of the world were forced by conscription to fight. He kept warning of Confederate raiding parties in the area who might steal their horses or burn their barns until Sophrena began to wonder if he too struggled with melancholy. After he fell silent, Sister Thelma said the hens had quit laying and there would be only mush and biscuits for the morning meal. Sophrena felt weighted down by their unhappy reports.

But then Brother Kenton began talking about how his spirit had been freed the first time he'd watched the Believers worship at Union village. That had been a mere year before. He'd once been married in the world, but his wife suffered from hysteria and had deserted him to return to the bosom of her mother.

He raised his hands up in front of him to study them before he continued speaking. "These hands were given the gift of healing by the good Lord above, but I had never properly lived for him. Something was always missing in my life. I thought it was the worldly love of a wife, but the spirit showed me otherwise. I shed the trappings of the world and embraced the simple life."

He had looked across the space between the lines of chairs and smiled directly at Sophrena. A simple smile that brought sunlight back into the room and made her forget all about hens that didn't lay eggs and guerilla raiding parties. She dropped her eyes to her hands folded in her lap, but she felt like spinning. And not to shake away the feeling. At that moment, it had not felt sinful. That came later upon recollection of the way her heart had leapt up at the sight of his smile. A smile that meant nothing more than brotherly love as was proper at a union meeting.

When it came her time to speak, her words came out with uncommon hesitancy as she reported on the number of hats the sisters had managed to weave in the week prior. Brother Jackson frowned and told her to speak up for he was hard of hearing, and Sister Emma asked if she might have caught a chill that was giving her a sore throat. At once Brother Kenton told her to come by the infirmary the next day so he could mix her a draught of medicine.

She had not gone to the infirmary. There was no need. Her throat was not sore, and she was wise enough not to purposely seek stumbling blocks. Later Eldress Lilith had taken her to task for not getting treatment for her throat ailment.

"A Shaker must keep her body whole in order to properly perform her duties to the best of her abilities," the eldress told her.

"Yea," Sophrena had agreed, and added to her sin by pretending her throat had gotten better overnight when it never ailed to begin with. Even little, unspoken lies wrapped around a person and trapped them in a web of untruth that was hard to escape.

The spring passed and summer brought many chores to keep her hands busy. Others were chosen to guide the novitiates for a season after she confessed her conflicted spirit to Eldress Lilith. An answer to prayers Sophrena had not thought to offer, for she was weary of keeping count of the faults of the new sisters. It was much better to work in the gardens. To plunge her hands into the dirt. To pluck out the weeds just as she needed to pluck out the weeds of discontent from her heart.

She went out to the gardens each day with willing hands, for it might not be many seasons before the piling on of years sapped her strength for such work. She picked strawberries and beans. She pulled onions, carrots, and beets. The sunshine on her shoulders and bonnet was welcome, and the sweat on her brow, earned and satisfying.

Back in the houses, she prayed at the proper times. She danced without missteps and kept her eyes away from the brethren's side of the meetinghouse. She hid her malaise except for confessing her lack of proper spirit to Eldress Lilith.

She could not keep all her sins secret. It was wrong to keep any of them secret, but one had to figure out what sin one was committing before one could confess it. At least that was the excuse she made for herself before the devil dug a hole to trip her up. Or if not the devil, some varmint.

Whichever, the hole in the garden row hidden by bean vines was her downfall. She stepped into the hole, twisted her ankle sideways, and fell headlong in the dirt, scattering the beans from her basket. Such a fall could not be hidden. Nor could she keep from gasping from the pain when she tried to stand.

Brother Kenton was called to the garden to determine if bones were broken. The only way to do that was by examination. After he carefully removed her shoe, his long fingers probed her ankle through her stocking. His hands cradled her foot as he gently bent it back and forth. Her breathlessness had not been completely from the pain caused by that movement. The flush on her cheeks not only from the summer sunshine.

He determined her ankle was not broken, only badly sprained. She spent three days in the infirmary with nothing to keep her mind occupied except the basket of hand sewing that was brought to her each morning. Brother Kenton said she must stay off her feet, but that didn't mean her hands could not work. Or that her eyes and ears would not be hearing and seeing the doctor as he went about his duty of tending to the sick.

Each day she was there, he checked her ankle, healing hands touching her skin with great gentleness. At other times, he came and leaned in the doorway for no other purpose than to ask how she was doing or to comment on how one of the other sisters or brothers was healing. Always smiling. Always cheerful. Always looking at her as though she mattered.

But of course, she mattered. All her brethren treasured her as a sister just as she treasured them. It was the way of the Believers. To love all the same. Whatever sickness of the spirit that was trying to overwhelm her was all that made her imagine anything different. That was what had planted in her head the idea that Brother Kenton was noticing her as Sophrena who wasn't yet too old to dance instead of simply Sister Sophrena who filled a spot on the far side of the meetinghouse.

On the second morning Sophrena was in the infirmary, Sister Edna brought a basket of dresses to be hemmed. When she passed Brother Kenton leaving Sophrena's room, she bent her head and muttered a morning greeting to his cheery hello. She watched him with a dark scowl as he left the room.

"That brother lacks the proper gravity." Sister Edna let out a huff of breath as she set the basket down with a thump beside Sophrena's chair.

"I should hope there's no rule against a cheerful heart." Sophrena shifted her foot on the cushiony pillow Brother Kenton had just brought her. "Is not that what we should all have as we go about our duties?"

Sister Edna turned her scowl on Sophrena. "A Believer needs to mind his duties with a serious demeanor and attention to his work. I should think especially a doctor who tends to the ill and injured. Brother Benjamin never went around with such a face."

"Brother Benjamin was generally of a good humor." Sophrena did not look at Sister Edna for fear the woman might note Sophrena's good humor and find fault in it. Instead she pulled one of the dresses out of the basket and arranged it on her lap before she picked up her needle.

"But he was not continually laughing like a child tickling his own nose with a hen's feather," Sister Edna said. "Such is not proper for a brother with the task of healing."

"I seem to recall reading a Bible verse in Proverbs about how a merry heart worketh good like a medicine. If so, then surely Brother Kenton will add power to his draughts with his happy ways."

Sophrena took great care in threading her needle and finding her thimble. When at last she did look up, Sister Edna's eyes were mere slits as she stared at Sophrena.

"If I were you, Sister Sophrena, I would be very careful which draughts of medicine you are hankering after. I sense sin is ready to overtake you."

"Nay, I pray not." Sophrena calmly turned up the hem on the dress sleeve before she looked up at Sister Edna. "The two of us have long been sisters together, so I know you will pray the same. Come back after the workday and I will have the sewing finished."

She had been glad to see Sister Edna go with her sour spirit, but as she hemmed the sleeve with tiny stitches, she knew Sister Edna was right. That was why, in spite of Brother Kenton saying she should rest her ankle for a full week, she had gone back out to the gardens after three days.

And now here she sat beside young Heather with a basket of sewing between them. Heather had asked to help and Sophrena did not have the heart to refuse her, even though she often had to pull out the girl's stitches after she had gone to bed to redo them on the morrow. The girl never knew since all the dresses were so alike. She wore one of them herself now. It looked unusual with the mound of baby growing under the skirt.

This time Sophrena could not leave to go back to the gardens to avoid being near Brother Kenton. As she made her stitches and listened to Heather talk of her husband, she could not be sure the devil was not throwing more temptations in her path. But what if it wasn't the devil's doing? What if it was the Lord knowing her need and answering her prayers?

She could believe Heather was that. God's plan. But what of Brother Kenton? He was a covenanted Believer. She was a covenanted Believer. Sometimes she paused in her sewing when such thoughts assaulted her and stared at the fire, but she found no answer in the flames.

15

*H*eather was glad of the hand sewing to keep her busy as she sat in front of the fire with Aunt Sophrena. That's how she thought of her, even though when she spoke her name aloud she said Sister Sophrena. In her mind she was aunt. Family. Heather needed family.

Sometimes an hour would go by without a word passing between them, but it was a comfortable silence. A necessary silence. The Shakers valued silence. While at first such silence had felt odd to Heather, as the days passed she began to be glad of the silent time that allowed her the privacy of thought. Sophrena didn't push Heather for words simply for the sake of dispelling the silence. Nor did she offer her own words. Often as she sat beside Heather and worked her needle through the cloth of whatever garment she held in her lap, she looked to be occupied with thoughts that were troubling, but she never spoke them aloud. Heather had no idea what could be burdening her aunt's heart, but she knew very well why her own heart was weighted down.

News of happenings out in the world did find its way to the Shaker village. Not particular news of Gideon, but general news of the war. General Sherman was marching on through the Southern states of Georgia and South Carolina toward the sea, but instead of pursuing him, the Confederate General Hood was moving his army to the northwest to challenge the Union forces in Nashville. Even though there was no news of fighting as yet, a battle was clearly in the offing.

The Shaker doctor carried that report to her. He was not like the other Shaker men who often hurried past the cabin with their eyes averted, as though worried they might catch a glimpse of her through a window or open door. The doctor, on the other hand, had a ready smile and no reluctance to take measure of the growth of the baby within her.

Brother Kenton, as he told her to call him, came by the cabin every day. Sometimes he came alone, which seemed to cause Sophrena great unease as if it was wrong for him to be there. After all, the Shakers did take great care to keep the men and women apart.

Sophrena had explained that was the reason for the two stairways in the Trustees' House. "As there are in every house where both brothers and sisters might have need to climb to an upper story."

Heather remembered Sister Muriel's quick removal of Heather's hand from the railing in that house. "But what could it hurt for the men and women to use the same stairs? Wouldn't that be simpler?" Sophrena had told her of the Shakers' desire for a simple life.

"Oh, nay, the simpler way is to keep away temptations of the flesh," Sophrena said. "The Ministry has determined such temptations can best be avoided by keeping the brothers and sisters from sharing the same space where there might be the chance of touching."

"But don't you dance?"

"Yea, we do indeed." Sophrena smiled over at Heather before looking back at her sewing. "But not as you must be imagining. Not as people of the world dance. Our dances are labors of love for the Lord above. We march in lines and circles and at times shake and whirl as the spirit falls upon us."

"But not together?" Heather was trying to picture such a dance.

"Yea, together in unity of movement and spirit." She looked over at Heather again. "But not by clinging to one another and inviting wrong thoughts into our minds instead of worshipful ones. If you want, you can come to meeting and see for yourself."

"That might be good," Heather said.

"Yea, you will see." Sophrena paused her needle and stared toward the fire before she added, "It is a good way."

Heather wasn't sure which of them she was trying most to convince—Heather or herself. Heather could not imagine ever being convinced of the need for such separation. Hadn't she lived among whole divisions of soldiers? She'd touched them many times when they brought their uniforms to her or when she helped care for the wounded after a battle without ever once feeling the temptation of the flesh that she felt simply looking into Gideon's eyes. That was the way the Lord intended. One man, one woman, two hearts promised to one another forever. And children to bless the union.

That too was something the Shakers did not sanction. No marriages. As a result, no babies. So she wasn't sure if it was Brother Kenton being in the cabin that caused Sophrena such uneasiness or if it was merely Heather's condition that his presence brought more to mind. Whichever, her aunt stayed apart whenever he was there, perhaps to be sure to avoid that forbidden touch of his hand or arm. Sometimes one of the eldresses, either Corinne, the one Heather had met on that first day, or a long-faced younger woman named Lilith, came with the doctor.

When they came, Sophrena would slip on her cloak and be gone from the cabin to fetch this or that need. Brother Kenton paid Sophrena's hasty departures no mind, nor did Eldress Corinne. But the other eldress would watch Sophrena go out the door with a frown sprouting between her eyebrows. The frown did not go away when the woman turned back to stand like a sentry over Brother Kenton while he asked Heather about pains and other signs of imminent birth.

Such talk made Eldress Lilith's frown darken and she often encouraged Brother Kenton to hurry his visit in order to see to his other patients. Heather had no difficulty divining the woman's underlying message that those patients would be proper Believers with more acceptable ailments.

Brother Kenton didn't let her words rush him, although he did seem to be more careful in what he said when the eldresses were with him than when he was alone with Heather and the silent Sophrena. With only the three of them in the cabin, he spent time trying to ease Heather's worries about the birthing process.

"Don't be concerned, Sister," he said on one of those mornings as he patted Heather's hand. "Babies generally come into the world with no difficulty at all. When I was still doctoring in the world, many were the times the babe would be wrapped in a blanket in his mother's arms before I reached the house. Birthing is a natural process. Not one without discomfort, I regret to say, but one with such rewards that most mothers dismiss the pains straightway for the joys of motherhood."

"I'm not afraid to give birth. I helped my mother when she had my little brothers," Heather said. "I will be glad when the time comes."

"Yea, as will I." He patted her hand again. "A birth is not something a Shaker doctor will often get the chance to attend, but seeing a new child of God take a first breath is one part of doctoring in the world I admit to missing. The miracle of birth." Then as though suddenly remembering Sophrena, who was busily wiping off the shelves she'd just cleaned earlier that morning, he glanced over at her. "Is that something you've ever shared, Sister Sophrena? Did you have children in the world?"

She paused in her dusting and stared down at the cloth in her hand before she said, "Nay."

Although he had to be aware that Sophrena was not comfortable with the talk of births, he went on. "Then you must attend your relative of the world when the time comes for her confinement. It will give you a whole new way of thinking of the Christ's birth in a stable and be a Christmas gift to you."

"A Believer has no need of gifts at Christmas," Sophrena said. "Our Mother Ann instead says we should give of our plenty to the poor at this time of the year."

"Yea, that is good." Brother Kenton put his hands on his knees and leaned forward in his chair toward Sophrena. "But that doesn't mean we can't rejoice in the unexpected gifts the good Lord showers down on us. This, our young sister's baby, will be one of those gifts. Not something we sought, but something we were given. A good thing."

"Not sinful?" Sophrena lifted her eyes to look directly at Brother Kenton. Then a flush crawled up into her cheeks as she glanced over at Heather beside him and added, "Forgive me, Sister Heather, I don't mean to be unkind, but in our Society, marriage is forbidden and thus the results of such unions as well."

"My baby is not sinful," Heather said, but without any resentment at her aunt's words. She could understand her unease with the thought of the marital union after so many years among the Shakers. "I am not one of your Society, Sister Sophrena. I will never be a Shaker if it means giving up the joy of family."

"We have family here," Sophrena said but with little enthusiasm in her voice.

Brother Kenton laughed. "That we do. Many brothers and sisters, but no daughters or sons. I did not mean to push wrong thinking toward you, Sister Sophrena. I am new to the Society while you have been a covenanted Believer many years. Even though I too have signed the covenant to follow the Believer's way, I cannot look upon the birth of a new child as sinful. You will see." He stood from his chair. "We will all see. And if I take too much joy into this step back into a more worldly kind of doctoring, I will confess such to Brother Ernest. He often tells me that I lack proper understanding of the Believers' rules."

"I know the rules well," Sophrena said softly as she went back to dusting the shelf that could not have had time to gather an iota of dirt.

"I am learning them," Brother Kenton said with steady cheer. "The same as I'm learning the dances, but I sometimes make a misstep there as I may have done so here in talking too much. Another of my sins Brother Ernest points out that I must shake from me."

"Worry not, Brother. We each have our own sins to confess and our Lord is quick to forgive them. We hold naught against you, do we, Sister Heather?"

"Of course not." Heather did not add how she was glad to hear that doubt lived in the minds of some of the Shakers as to their beliefs. Doubt she was beginning to note in her aunt in spite of Sophrena's determined words defending the Shaker way.

"That is good to hear," the doctor said. "Be sure to send for me if anything changes, young sister. I do have to warn you that most babies tend to come into the world in the middle of the night as did the Christ child."

"And angels sang in the night sky to the shepherds," Heather said.

"Yea, so they did," Brother Kenton said. "And you will be singing to your wee little one before Christmas Day if my eyes do not deceive me."

After the doctor left, Heather looked at Sophrena. "You don't really believe my baby is sinful, do you, Aunt Sophrena?" She realized after she spoke that she had forgotten to say "sister," but she didn't change her words.

Sophrena didn't seem to notice. She was still staring toward the door that had closed behind Brother Kenton. "Nay. Nay, I do not."

"Will you have to confess that to the eldress?" Heather knew Sophrena continued to visit the Centre House to make such confessions to Eldress Lilith.

"Perhaps," Sophrena said. Then the bell was sounding from the center of the village to signal the midday meal. Sophrena shook herself a bit before she carefully folded her dusting cloth and tucked it away. "It is time to go get our food."

As the days passed, Shaker sisters brought gifts to Sophrena and Heather. Shawls to keep them warm since the cabin wasn't as well built as the houses. Squares of flannel for when the baby came. A few of these women showed the same mixture of uneasiness and eagerness in regard to Heather's condition as Sophrena. Some were mothers. Others, like Sophrena, had never borne children.

Even if their children were still among the Shakers, such relationships were ignored. The children lived in a children's house and the mothers were now sisters to their sons and daughters. That was something Heather would never understand no matter how many ways it was explained to her.

Sophrena gave Heather a book about the Shakers' Mother Ann and let her read for herself how the woman determined through prayers and visions that the deaths of her four infants were a sign to her she should not have married. She believed the Lord was leading her into a better way of life where she could live as those in heaven lived. Without acrimony. Without the stress of individual family life. Without wars and conflicts. With simple peace. One way to obtain that peace was to allow the spirit to overtake one's body and shake away all sin, but true worship was best expressed in working with one's hands and giving one's heart to God.

Heather tried not to condemn their ways simply because they seemed so strange to her, but at times, she did want to ask what of Mary, the mother of Jesus, who had pondered in her heart the amazing child she'd borne? Was she not blessed with other children given to her in the natural way? And what of Hannah who had begged the Lord for a child with such ardor the priest had thought she was drunk on wine? Had not the Lord blessed her prayer and given her the desires of her heart? Children were gifts from God. Her baby the same as Hannah's in the Bible so long ago.

If Sophrena noted Heather's frowns when she was explaining something about the Shaker way, she didn't comment on it. In fact, there were times while she spoke of their beliefs that her own forehead would pucker with the lines of a frown. Whether that was due to the words she was saying or the dim light for her sewing, Heather could not be sure.

It wasn't due to any argument Heather voiced. She bit her lip and kept quiet. These people were giving her shelter without asking anything in return except that she consider their ways. Not that she would ever have the first thought of becoming a Shaker. She was only pausing here until Gideon returned. And that only because her father had turned her away from his door.

She wrote Beth and Gideon with no assurance that either would read her letters. She could imagine her father pitching her letter into the fire, and who knew if a letter would have the chance to catch up with the army. If Gideon wrote to her, his letter would go to the farm. Until he received a letter from her, he would have no way to know she'd been forced to find another refuge.

So she waited. For the baby. For Gideon. For the sorrow for her mother and brothers to lessen. For her anger at her father to stop stabbing through her. Now and again, she would remember her mother's words asking her to forgive, but how could she when he'd barred her from her own home?

16

Gideon straightened from setting up his tent and stared across the field. Snow. That really was snow spitting through the air and hitting him in the face. As if war by itself wasn't bad enough, the weather had to continually find ways to add to his misery. So hot in the summer a man could die from lack of water. So cold in the winter that a chicken roosting house looked like a fine hotel. Plenty of houses around the city of Nashville, but Captain Hopkins ordered them to stay together and ready. An officer couldn't be searching through a hundred houses looking for his men when it was time to go out against the enemy. The captain wasn't one to mess with.

Gideon turned up the collar of his coat and pulled it tighter around him. He cast his eye about, to see if he could spot anything that might make a fire. Thousands of other soldiers settling into camp inside the city's fortifications were no doubt doing the same.

The armies were gathering. Union tents blanketed the space around Gideon. Out beyond the fortifications, scouts reported the Confederates were massing troops on the hills around Nashville. Down the river, Confederate ships set up battlements to block the

Union supply boats. The booms of that confrontation came to them like distant thunder, but here, closer to hand, there were no signs of imminent action. General Thomas, the Rock of Chickamauga, was in command of the troops, and Pap never got in a hurry. That was fine with Gideon. He wasn't the least bit anxious to be lining up to fight except maybe to get it over with. The battle would have to be fought, but when was out of Gideon's hands. He, along with the other soldiers, was settling in to wait for the officers to give the orders.

At least food was in plentiful supply. Most everything was in plentiful supply with Nashville full of profiteers ready to take a soldier's army pay with temptations across the board. The place teemed with chances for trouble, but Captain Hopkins kept a tight rein on his men and ordered them to stay in camp. That was fine with Gideon. Better to stay away from temptation and remember his Heather Lou. He wasn't about to squander his pay on gambling, drinking, or any kind of rabble-rousing. Not when he was about to be a father.

The snow blew past him, leaving hard crystals of white gathered in the tent folds. After he and some others pooled their wood to get a fire going, Gideon sat beside it to write Heather. Just thinking of her made the fire feel warmer. The other men started a game of dice, but he paid them little attention as he wrote.

> *My sweet Heather Lou. I'm missing you something awful, but I'll be seeing you soon. Nothing can keep me away from you. We made camp on the outskirts of Nashville. The place puts me some in mind of Washington. Not as big, but with plenty of things going on that wouldn't be fit for your ears or eyes. Some fellow staggered by here all glassy-eyed a while ago and said a man could find anything he wanted over in that town. I'm thinking he might have wanted too much. He wasn't one of our company and a good thing. The Captain would have give him what for. He let us all know we were to*

stay in camp. Said we were here to beat back Johnny Reb and not to be losing our pay, not to mention our honor, to them scoundrels what cheat at cards or try to entice a man into sinning with strong drink or painted ladies. You don't have to be worrying none about me doing any of that, Heather Lou. You're the only girl I want, but I sure am missing you. Old Jake just ain't as good company in the middle of the night. Ha Ha.

Gideon squeezed the last line on the very bottom of the page. He looked at what he'd written. He hadn't even told her he loved her. He turned the page around and began writing on the side edges.

It's cold as anything here and my feet are wet. I need you praying for me. I'm not all that good at praying back for you, but I'll give it a try. I remember how you used to tell me praying's not hard. That the good Lord don't need fancy words or even words spoke out loud. That he already knows a man's heart. If he does, he knows I love you.

When he got all that written, he barely had room to squeeze in his initial at the bottom of the letter.

Jake, who'd been keeping the fire going, laughed when he glanced over and saw every inch of the page covered with writing. "You're a man of many words."

"I didn't say it all." With a sheepish grin, Gideon folded the letter. "But maybe I can write her again tomorrow."

"Tomorrow the captain will have us marching in circles just to keep us out of trouble."

"Might be a good thing. Leastways it might keep us warm." He stuck the letter in his pocket and held both hands out toward the fire. "I thought we went south."

"Winter must have trailed along with us," Jake said. "But think of it, lad. If us northerners are suffering, think how much more those southern boys are feeling the cold. They'll be sprouting icicles, but not us. We've seen plenty worse. A little spitting snow is hardly worth noticing. Now, is it?"

"But snow." Gideon shivered. "And if that wind would just quit blowing."

"Would be a blessing." A distant boom made Jake raise his head and listen. "Sounds like they're still going at it."

Gideon looked to the west. "Sundown will quiet them down soon."

"Never had any desire to do my fighting on a boat." Jake looked back at the fire. "Prefer my feet on the ground."

The Rebels had won the fight on the river the day before, but now Union ships had gone out to break through the barricade.

"At least they're fighting and not just freezing their toes off for nothing." Gideon pulled off one of his shoes and rubbed his toes. The sock was damp.

Jake frowned over at him. "You got to keep those feet dry, lad. Foot rot can ruin a man."

"Don't I know it." Heather had kept him in dry socks while she'd been with him. Carried them inside her dress pressed against her bosom. But now Heather was gone and his every sock carried the damp chill of the day.

He held his foot out toward the fire as another boom sounded. If he was on those boats, he might have more to worry about than foot rot. At least so far on this day, nobody was shooting at him.

"I can still march." He propped his shoe up by the fire. He thought it best to take off only one shoe at a time. A man could put one shoe on in a run, but not two.

"That's a good thing, because they'll be finding us a hill to charge up. Seems like we could fight on some nice flat ground with strong rock fences to take cover behind now and again." Jake leaned forward to poke at the fire.

"Captain says the Rebs aren't dummies. They take the high ground when they can, same as we would if we had the chance."

Gideon looked away to the south where the Confederate army was digging in on that high ground.

"I know. Always a hill a man has to charge up."

"Maybe this one will have trees." He could hope, Gideon thought.

"Could be." Jake picked up a twig and chewed on the end. "Trouble is, even if there are trees, a man can't stay behind them. Not and hang on to any honor."

"Honor." Gideon echoed. "A fine-sounding word."

"That it is," Jake agreed. "But it's beginning to wear a wee bit thin for some of us that have marched behind it up too many hills."

"We've gone up our share." Gideon stared at the fire and wished night would fall so the booming would stop. Too soon he'd be hearing more of those cannon booms once General Thomas gave the order to move.

Jake threw his twig in the fire. The end he'd been chewing sizzled, then burned and was gone. "A man can lag behind and not be the first man up the hill when he's got a baby he aims to see."

"Sounds like something my Heather Lou would say." Gideon leaned down and rubbed the toe of his sock. It felt a little drier. "She ask you to tell me that?"

"No, lad. I come up with the advice all on my own." Jake stared at the fire a long minute before he pushed up from the block of wood he'd been sitting on. "And good advice it is. A man doesn't always have to be the hero."

"A soldier without honor doesn't have much."

Jake looked down at him. "You could be right, lad, but a dead man has even less."

"Heather would tell you different. She'd say a man can always look to eternity."

"That he can. And a fine place we're promised it will be, but I'm thinking on dwelling here in this world a bit longer. If we can bear the weather." Jake grinned as he grasped Gideon's shoulder and gave it a little shake. "Keep that in mind when the time comes, lad, and stick with me. I'll get you through."

"You gonna get me through this weather?" Gideon asked.

"That could be a little harder." Jake stared off toward the western horizon. "My bones tell me it's going to be worse before it's better. We'll be fighting in the snow."

But it wasn't snow that fell on them a few days later while the generals were plotting their strategies. The snow changed to rain and then froze. The ice coated every surface and knocked down a fair number of tents. Captain Hopkins relented and let the men make their way across the ice-covered ground to barns, sheds, houses, any building with a roof to keep the ice from coating them the way it was everything else.

When daylight came the next morning, Gideon looked out at a glittering icy world and knew nobody would be fighting anybody but old man winter on this day. He didn't know whether to be relieved or sorry. It might be good to just get it over with.

17

*T*he weather was cold for early December. Heather even spotted snowflakes when she stepped out to the privy. She didn't walk about the village. Sophrena thought it better if she didn't wander around in her condition. Heather wasn't sure if that was because of concern for her or worry that the Shaker people might be offended by the sight of her growing shape that not even the fullest skirt could hide.

Brother Kenton said the baby growing was good, but sometimes Heather noted the hint of a frown that accompanied his words. She'd witnessed her mother's labor to push Lucas and Jimmy out into the world. She'd gripped Heather's hands so tightly during some of the pains that Heather's fingers had been bruised and sore for days. Mrs. Saunders, the neighborhood midwife, had encouraged her with soft words and gentle hands. That's who Heather had imagined helping her birth her baby. Her mother and Mrs. Saunders. But that was not to be. Instead she would have to depend on Sophrena, who appeared uneasy with the very thought of a baby, much less the messy job of bringing that baby into

119

the world. She might just faint dead away and Heather would be without help at all.

When Heather had those thoughts, she squared her shoulders and cradled the round form of the baby growing within her. If that happened, she was strong. Hadn't she followed after an army? Hadn't she done that for love? Love made hard things easier and she loved this little being inside her. She loved him so much she could do whatever had to be done to give him life.

Besides, Sophrena was like Heather's mother. She was like Heather herself. The same blood ran through them all, a powerful connection in spite of Sophrena having removed herself from the family fold. Heather felt the connection every time she looked directly into Sophrena's eyes. Sophrena felt it too. Heather was sure she did, no matter what she said about the way Shakers believed in a different type of family.

The snow turned to ice and pecked against the windows. But inside the cabin, the fire was warm and the lamps were lit. Food was on the table. All supplied by the Shaker people and carried to the cabin by Sophrena. The two of them sewed together. They ate together. They prayed in silence together, each in her own way, but to the same heavenly Father. They slept in the same room, their breaths mingling in the night air like Heather's and Beth's had before she had gone with Gideon.

It mattered not that they talked little and then only of the Shaker beliefs or of how winter was coming early or of the stitches they were making in the unending baskets of sewing. The bond was growing between them nevertheless. She would not desert Heather in her hour of need. Instead she had deserted her way of life to care for Heather. What could make one do that other than love?

And Gideon would come back to Heather. Her prayers would keep him safe and love would bring him back into her arms.

With ice tinkling against the window glass, they ate their night meal Sophrena had had the foresight to fetch early before the ice accumulated. Then as had become their custom, they returned to the chairs by the fire and went back to their sewing until the retiring bell.

On her first days in the village, Sophrena had explained the purpose of each ringing of the bell as it signaled the proper times for different activities. Rising in the morning and retiring at night. Times of rest and prayers. Meals. It tolled for the gathering to worship in their meetinghouse. Heather had come to depend on the bells to give her days rhythm. Up in the morning, eating and praying and sewing, to bed at night.

But all she was really doing was awaiting her time. Pondering this child in her heart as surely the mother of the Christ had once done so long ago. Wondering what lay ahead. Heather's child was not the miracle the Christ child was, come to save a sinful world. But her child was a gift to cherish. A miracle of love for her.

Heather no longer helped Sophrena with hemming the Shaker clothes. Instead she hemmed small squares of cloth for the baby's wrapping blankets and made him gowns of the soft cream-colored fabric one of the sisters had woven especially for that purpose and brought by the cabin earlier in the week.

"A sister or brother needs something to wear no matter how small that sister or brother might happen to be," Sister Doreen told Heather with a peek over her shoulder, as though worried someone might be listening who would find fault with her words. She let her gaze settle on Sophrena as she went on. "Don't you agree, Sister Sophrena?"

"Yea, the babe will need clothes." Sophrena looked up from fingering the material with a smile that seemed to put the other woman at ease.

Sister Doreen was short and tending toward roundness. The hair that peeked out below her cap was white, but her eyes carried the twinkle of perennial youth. She never came by the cabin without a gift and without bringing cheer through the door. Something Sophrena seemed to need even more than Heather as the days passed. Although she never complained of being isolated with Heather in the cabin, she had to be missing the companionship of the Shaker sisters she had lived with so long.

This night, with the ice enclosing them and shutting away the world outside the cabin, Sophrena seemed more relaxed in her talking, as if she didn't have to worry about an improper word being overheard. They spoke of the weather and of how Gideon's division would be in the south where the air would be warmer.

"Rain is not good either," Heather said.

"But kinder than ice, I would think," Sophrena said without looking up from her sewing. She had finished the basket of assigned sewing and was stitching a gown cut from Sister Doreen's soft cloth. Her stitches were much quicker than Heather's and the gown was taking shape under her skilled fingers.

"My Gideon never seemed to know how to keep dry." Heather frowned. "His feet especially. I took care to keep him in clean socks while I was with him, but now I am not with him."

"A good thing." Sophrena looked over at her. "In your condition. It is good you are here. Perhaps we can knit him some socks and send them to him."

Heather dropped her sewing and stared at the fire, barely hearing Sophrena's words. "But I miss him so much."

If only she could get a letter from him to know he was all right.

18

I fear your relative from the world is pulling you away from us, Sister Sophrena." Eldress Lilith made the dreaded clicking sound with her tongue as she narrowed her eyes on Sophrena.

Sophrena met her look for a few seconds before dropping her gaze to her hands folded in her lap. She was not sure how to respond. Was it young Heather pulling her from the Shaker way or her unwise feelings for Brother Kenton? Feelings that Brother Kenton gave no sign of noticing or sharing. At the thought, tears pricked at her eyes, but she blinked them away. It would surely compound her sin to allow Eldress Lilith to think she was showing remorse for the lacks the eldress was pointing out to her when her sorrow was simply an addition to her sin.

"Have you no wrongs to confess on this day?" Eldress Lilith prodded her when Sophrena stayed silent.

"I have many wrongs," Sophrena said softly as she raised her eyes to look past Eldress Lilith's head, out the window. Traces of ice lingered on the tree limbs in the shadow of the building, but most of it had glittered brilliantly in the burst of sunlight that had followed on the heels of the storm the next day and melted away.

If only the feelings within her heart giving her such unease would do the same. Glitter brightly for a short time and then burn away under the light of the spirit so her peace could be restored.

"A Believer must voice those wrongs in order to receive forgiveness." The eldress tapped her fingers on the narrow table between them with growing impatience.

So Sophrena borrowed her wrongs. "I am often impatient. I wish my work done more quickly than it can be done. I tire of the sameness of my sewing tasks. I was too quick with my prayers last night when the floor was chill under my knees. I had a wrong thought against one of my sisters." Sophrena stopped. No need in adding that her wrong thought just occurred when she had noted Eldress Lilith's impatience.

The eldress drummed her fingers on the table yet again as she silently considered Sophrena's list of sins. Sophrena was beginning to feel concern that she was divining her true sins that could not be spoken aloud. At least not to one so unforgiving as Eldress Lilith.

She wondered if the young sisters she had once prodded to confess their wrongs had hidden their true concerns in fear of her sternness. She sent up a prayer that it had not been so, for she would not have wanted to deny those sisters the opportunity to confess and receive proper forgiveness.

But can't you go directly to the Lord to ask forgiveness? Heather's words slid through Sophrena's mind. The girl had no interest in the Shaker way. She was wrapped completely around the new life growing inside her. She wanted family with every inch of her being the way Sophrena had once sought and found peace among her brothers and sisters here at Harmony Hill.

And now she had lost that peace by allowing carnal thoughts to burrow into her mind. Wrong thoughts of worldly love that she had once condemned in weaker-willed sisters. She did not imagine she was in love with Brother Kenton. That would be extremely foolish. But she could not deny she was wondering what it would be like if she were to love him in the way of the world. Nor could she deny he drew her eyes and caused her heart to beat oddly in her chest. She seemed unable to talk sensibly when he came to the cabin to check on Heather, and her cheeks continually felt warm in a way they did not after he left.

She thought of dear Jessamine again and the girl's curiosity about everything of the world. She had not regretted Jessamine leaving Harmony Hill to go to the world. The girl was not meant to be a Shaker, but Sophrena was. She was happy with her sisters. She was happy with the Believer's love. She needed nothing more. At least she had not until she turned fifty and Brother Kenton came to Harmony Hill.

Eldress Lilith had been silent for a long time. Not a good thing. Sophrena cast around for some other wrong for which to ask forgiveness. Perhaps her weariness of spirit.

She started to speak, but the eldress held up a hand to stop her. "Nay, Sister Sophrena. Do not add words simply for the sake of filling the air between us with noise. That makes nothing better."

"Yea, you are right," Sophrena agreed meekly.

"Sacrifice Day is almost upon us. I will expect you to spend the day in prayer and contemplation of your shortcomings. If you have aught against a sister or brother, you must go to them and heal that breach."

"Yea, I will do so."

"Even Sister Edna?"

"Yea, if I have erred against her, but I have not seen her since I began caring for Sister Heather."

"Oh?" Eldress Lilith raised her eyebrows as if Sophrena's words surprised her. "Sister Edna tells me she sees you often."

Sophrena frowned as she tried to remember when she'd last seen the sister. "Then she must be watching from a distance." That wasn't surprising. Sister Edna had always been a watcher. One intent on observing others to be sure they were keeping their feet on the Shaker way. Such a duty was needed at times, but Sophrena was glad it had never been her duty.

"Yea, that could be," Eldress Lilith agreed with a slight motion of her hand. "Whether you saw her or not is of no consequence. What matters is what she saw. She tells me Brother Kenton goes to the cabin almost every day and sometimes twice."

"Sister Heather's time is near. He is keeping a close watch upon her."

"Yea, so it seems." Eldress Lilith clicked her tongue with disapproval. "Sister Edna says he appears to enjoy those visits."

Sophrena pulled in a little breath and hoped the eldress wouldn't notice the stain of red climbing into her cheeks. "Our brother has a cheerful way." She had to bite her lip to keep from adding that Sister Edna did not. "Such has been a blessing to our young sister as she hopes for delivery of a healthy baby. That is her prayer."

"One that might not be answered."

Sophrena looked at the eldress in surprise. "Brother Kenton thinks all will be well."

"I'm sure you do remember Mother Ann lost all her babies as young children. The Lord speaks truth to us in many ways." The eldress clicked her tongue again. "Or finds ways to punish our wrong thinking."

"I will pray he chooses other ways to correct our wrongs," Sophrena said softly.

"Yea, that would be well. It would be good if you also prayed for right thinking and willing service." She pushed up from her chair.

Sophrena stood quickly. "I will make that prayer."

"Good. At meeting tomorrow you can shake away the carnal thinking that seems to be chasing after you, Sister Sophrena. Bring the young sister with you. Perhaps the spirit will fall upon her and reveal to her the error of her ways."

Sophrena had no belief that would happen. In truth, she had no wish for it to happen. She didn't want Heather to deny her love for her soldier husband or to be ready to surrender the baby to other sisters to raise. There was something too beautiful about the girl sitting by the fire, closing away everything around her as she looked inward toward her unborn child.

But what of salvation? Had she not accepted the Shaker life long ago as the way to salvation? Could it be that the Millennial rules and what was written in the Covenant she had signed were wrong? Sophrena sighed as the questions circled in her head. What was the truth?

I am the way, the truth, the life. The Christ's words from the Good Book slipped into her head. But what of Mother Ann and her teachings? Sophrena had embraced them along with the Bible teachings for many years. She had gone forth in worship and found joy in the dance. She had shaken free of worldly trappings. Or thought she had. Perhaps she had never truly conquered the lust for things of the world. Not things. Feelings. Carnal love. A seed buried deep in her heart and now watered by her attraction to Brother Kenton.

The next morning, she was up before the rising bell and tiptoed out of the sleeping room to keep from waking Heather. She poked up the coals of the fire and added wood. Then she knelt in front of the flames to ask forgiveness for all the sins she had been unable to voice aloud to Eldress Lilith. She prayed for skillful hands to help Heather when the birthing time came. Then she stopped pushing words up in her mind and instead bent her head. The fire crackled as the flames wrapped around the new wood, but in spite of that, the silence fell about her in a profound and isolating way. Heather was in the next room. Her Shaker brothers and sisters were spread about her in various other buildings, but at that moment she felt completely alone. Starkly alone.

Only one other time did she remember feeling so alone. Bereft of love. Bereft of hope. That was before she had come to Harmony Hill. Even now, after so many years, she could remember how passionately she had prayed for the Lord to show her a way to survive in the dark valley of her union with Jerome. Not even a week passed after that prayer before they came to the Shaker village. And the Lord had blessed her with joy in the love of her sisters and purpose in the pleasing work of her hands.

It had been enough, more than enough. A blessed answer to a

desperate prayer. Why now had she stepped back into that lonely valley? She was not alone. She had much love all around her. In spite of that, discontent had sprouted in her heart. Eldress Lilith would tell her that was because she had allowed a splinter of worldliness to fester there. She should have shaken such feelings away long before now. Perhaps the eldress was right. In a few hours when the meeting bell rang she would go forth to labor the songs. She would sweep aside temptation and put the devil behind her. She would ready herself for Sacrifice Day when she could cleanse her spirit to better celebrate the birth of the Christ.

"Show me the proper way, dear Lord. Rid me of sin and pluck temptation's weed from my heart," she mouthed the words silently.

"Are you all right, Sister Sophrena?"

Sophrena jumped at the sound of Heather's voice. She had been so deep in prayer she had been unaware of the girl coming into the room.

"Forgive me, Sister Sophrena. I should not have disturbed your prayers, but when you gave no notice of hearing the rising bell, I was concerned."

"The rising bell?" Sophrena looked toward the window as she got to her feet. "Are you sure it rang?"

"Yes, very sure," Heather moved closer to the fire. "It wakes me every dawn."

"Yea, so it does, but I didn't hear it."

"You must have been listening for the Lord's voice instead," Heather said.

"Yea, a needful part of prayer." Sophrena added wood to the fire and watched sparks fly up the chimney. A waste of proper heat.

"Did he speak to you?"

"The Lord speaks in many ways. Perhaps I will hear him at meeting today." Sophrena turned toward Heather. "Our meetings are not open to those of the world during the winter season, but since you are living among us, Eldress Lilith suggested you might want to attend to ponder your own feelings for the Lord as we sing."

"I can no longer hide the swell of the baby within me," Heather said.

"Things are not to be hidden in our worship. Whatever the need, that is where the songs take us."

"I will not be expected to dance, will I?" Heather looked concerned.

"Nay." Sophrena laughed. "Many of the dances take much practice. You can only watch, but if you tarry with us, I will teach you some of the steps should you want to try our way of worship."

"What is the purpose of the dances?" Heather asked.

"To move closer to the Lord and rid oneself of sin."

"You Shakers worry a lot about sin."

"Do you not do the same in the world?" Sophrena frowned over at Heather.

"It is not necessary for us to name them every one."

"Does that not make your errors harder to recognize and easier to pile the dust of yesterday over them?"

"At times," Heather admitted, then added with a smile. "Such would surely be hard to do in this place. I have not seen a speck of dust since I came here."

"It is good to sweep clean our houses and our spirits. You will see." Sophrena laid another piece of wood on the fire before she reached for her cloak. "Rest here by the fire while I fetch our morning meals and then we will get ready for our meeting. A person open to the spirit can find much simple joy in our songs."

"Will the songs be familiar to my ears?" Heather lowered herself into the chair by the fire.

"Not to your ears, but perhaps to your heart."

Sophrena went out the door into the crisp air of the morning with the lines of one of the songs playing through her head. *'Tis a gift to be simple. 'Tis a gift to be free.*

Free. Was she free?

19

*A*fter they ate, Sophrena ushered Heather inside the meet-inghouse to what she called the visitors' bench just as the gathering bell sounded.

"You must stay seated and not interfere with the exercise of the songs," Sophena instructed.

When Heather promised to do as told, Sophrena heeded the call of the bell and hastened out the door.

Heather rested her head against the wall. She was so tired. Her back hurt and her feet were swelling against the lacings of her shoes. She would have been content to stay by the fire and read the Bible on this Sunday morning. But Sophrena had been eager to go to meeting and have Heather accompany her. Heather could bear the hard bench and the stiff wall behind her back for a while. She almost whispered a prayer that the meeting would not go on over-long, but bit back the words. Such a prayer would not be proper. Worship was worth a little discomfort.

She wondered if Beth and the boys would be heading to church with their father for spiritual renewal on this morning. Dear Beth. Heather thought of the letter she'd received from her a few days ago. Could Beth be right in thinking her father was feeling remorse for his unkindness? Beth claimed that was so, but Heather could not forget his cold look as he sent her away.

She turned her mind away from her father. Better to send her prayers toward Gideon who might even now be in a conflict with the Rebels. War did not take time off for the Sabbath.

Heather shifted on the hard bench and waited. She knew not for what, but even inside the big empty building there was a feel of anticipation as the bell continued to toll. Then the ringing stopped and a Sunday kind of silence fell around her, as though not just Heather but the whole village was waiting for whatever was going to happen next.

Church, she supposed, but nothing in the large open room brought to mind anything about church. Rows of benches were lined on either side of an open space in the middle of the floor. The winter light spilled in through tall windows onto the polished broad floor planks. No curtains or shades hindered the light and no rugs softened the harsh bareness of the room. Easier to keep clean, Heather supposed, remembering how the Shakers couldn't abide dirt.

But other things that seemed necessary to worship were not in evidence either. No preacher podium. No table for a Bible or offering plates. No song books. No piano. Not the first hint of decoration of any kind, not even a sprig of Christmas greenery. At the church back home, a few of the ladies would have already tied red ribbons around cedar branches to decorate the windowsills and Mrs. Fenton would have fashioned a couple of wreaths of greenery and bittersweet berries or mistletoe for the doors.

Here there was nothing. Even the white walls were bare except for the same type of blue strips of pegs circling the room she'd noted in that other building when she'd first come to the village. No chairs were hung upside down on these. All the pegs were empty except for a candleholder by one of the doors. Identical small iron stoves stood at either end of the room. Heather considered moving to a bench closer to the stove nearest her since the room was chilly, but she stayed where she was. She'd promised Sophrena. Besides, the silence was so profound that even the squeaking complaint of her bench as she shifted to get more comfortable sounded too loud.

Something clicked like a door opening, but the outside doors were still closed as were the two blue doors at either end of the room. Sophrena had told her those selected for the Ministry lived above the meeting room. Another slight click drew Heather's eyes to a two-inch square door easing open above one of the inside doors.

She was not alone as she had imagined. Eyes were peering through the opening. Heather sneaked a look toward the other end of the room. Eyes were peering out of an opening above that door too, pinning her down on the bench as surely as if hands had reached out to hold her there. The eyes weren't friendly. They weren't unfriendly. They just were. Observing. Judging.

Heather was glad when the silence was broken by the muted sounds of singing. Then the outside doors were swinging open and the Shakers fell silent as they entered the building. The women through one door. The men, the other. Their feet made only a whisper of sound as they went across the floor to the benches, the women to her right and the men to her left. They kept filing into the room. Too many for Heather to keep count.

Only a very few let their eyes stray toward her even after they were standing silently in front of the benches. Heather looked up at the openings above the doors. The eyes there were no longer on her but instead watched the men and women standing silently in front of the benches.

Sophrena was one of the last to enter the building. Even though Heather had been watching for her, she almost hadn't picked her out. The women all looked so the same in their like dresses with the bonnets covering their heads. But it was more than their dress. It was the way they moved and how they stood. Different heights. Different sizes, but in spite of that, so alike.

At a signal she did not catch, the men and women sat down.

133

All at the same time. Sophrena had told her that unity in action led to unity in spirit. It put Heather in mind of the army companies marching in step, obedient to the officers' directions. Not so strange. She had often heard a preacher speak of the army of God. Soldiers for Christ.

She shut her eyes and thought of her soldier, Gideon. Would she ever see him again? The baby jumped inside her as though to protest her worry. She bent her head and prayed for Gideon, for them both, for them all three. She might be inside a church much different than anything she'd ever imagined, but it was still a church. A place for prayer.

A gray-haired man stepped into the center of the room between the rows of benches and began to speak. He was very thin with stooped shoulders, but when he spoke, his deep voice commanded the attention of every person in the room.

"Sacrifice Day, a time for atonement, is near. Search within yourself for every wrong. No sin is too small to be repented and plucked from our hearts. Heaven knows no sin and here at Harmony Hill we are bringing heaven down among us. Each wrong, each error in our walk, must be swept away, for good spirits will not abide where there is sin. Prepare for perfect reconciliation one with another. All grudges, hard feelings, and disaffection toward any brother or sister must be left behind. Be ready to beg forgiveness from your brethren, from your sisters, from the Eternal Father. Prepare your spirits to start afresh, for nothing which is settled on Sacrifice Day can ever be brought forward against another of your holy family. If one has done any harm, imagined or real, toward you, offer forgiveness fully and completely. An unforgiving spirit is not a Believer's way."

Heather hardly dared breathe. Her mother's words seemed to be coming out of this man's mouth straight at her. Forgive.

The Shaker man let his eyes circle around the room, landing on this or that person to perhaps prod those he knew had most need of his words. Then as if her mother were directing his eyes, he looked straight at Heather, seeming to demand she hear and heed his words. She was relieved when he turned back to the Shakers.

"Remember our Mother Ann's words. Labor to make the way of God your own. Let it be your inheritance, your treasure, your occupation, your daily calling." He lifted his hands into the air and stood in silence a moment before he went on. "Now let us go forth to labor these songs with our spirits in tune with the Lord's. May we be open to receive whatever gift of the spirit falls down upon us."

He stepped back to his place by the bench and the other Shakers all rose to stand with him. Then they were moving aside the benches with eagerness. When the floor was cleared, one of the women began singing. Not words, but sounds. A few other sisters and then some of the men joined in as though the song was as familiar to them as a hymn would have been to the people at Heather's church.

The Shakers began moving up and back and in circles to the sound of the voices. Part marching, part dancing as they moved to the rhythm of the song. The singers increased the speed of their wordless songs. The line dancers reversed and passed in and out and circled without touching. Their shoes whispered against the floor and the fabric of the dresses swished as they passed by Heather so close she could have touched them. She kept her hands tucked under her cloak. The singing changed, and Heather was relieved to hear words she could understand.

> "Come old and young, come great and small.
> There's love and union free for all,
> And everyone that will obey
> Has now a right to dance and play."

They did seem to be playing. Smiles lit up their faces as they sang. Some of the sisters began to skip. Even some of the older women with gray hair peeking out from under their bonnets. Round and round they went. All at once the mood changed. Somebody shouted a warning about the devil and feet began stomping to chase him away from their worship.

135

Heather's bench jarred and bounced her back against the wall. She moved her hand out to embrace the swell of her baby. She wasn't sure if she was protecting him from the threat of the devil in the room or the fury of the Shakers ridding themselves of even the thought of evil.

As suddenly as it started, the stomping stopped with the dancers gliding past as they pretended to sweep every corner. The song changed and with it the mood yet again. A man yelled. A woman screamed and began to tremble all over. Another began to whirl. The hysteria raced through the dancers until more than half of them were whirling and shaking or shouting.

Heather tried not to show her astonishment. Their worship was like nothing she could have ever imagined. That they danced was no surprise. Everybody knew Shakers worshiped by dancing. And it was common knowledge they were given to tremors of the spirit that shook their bodies. After all, they weren't called Shakers without reason.

But Heather had never actually thought about how that shaking might look. Frantic and noisy, without order. Certainly nothing at all like any church service she'd ever witnessed. Even the impromptu gatherings of men out in the open in the army camps had more of a feeling of church than whatever was happening here in the Shakers' meetinghouse.

Then one of the women spun in front of her in such frenzy that she fell to the floor. Heather was not too sure she might not join her in a swoon. Where before the room had felt chill, now it was too warm with so many whirling bodies. The eggs and biscuits she had eaten not so long ago were beginning to swirl in her stomach. She gripped the bench, willing herself to keep a steady head. Another sister fell prostrate. None of the others seemed to notice.

Heather looked through the whirling people for Shakers she'd met. Brother Kenton had a smile spread across his face as he moved his feet with abandon in a way that made her think of the jigs she'd seen in the army camps. Eldress Lilith had lost the shadow of dis-

approval that generally darkened her face and peered heavenward
with a look of deep contentment. There was Sister Doreen who
had brought her the material for the baby's gowns. It was no surprise that she was whirling like a child. But where was Sophrena?

At last she spotted her standing very still in the middle of the floor
with her hands reaching toward the ceiling. She seemed unaware
of the fervor of the others spinning around her. She was praying.
Heather had no doubt of that, and although she had no idea what
her prayers were, she sent her own prayers out to join them. Prayers
without words just as the Shakers' first songs had been sounds
without meaning. A prayer could have meaning without words.

As though those prayers touched Sophrena, she lowered her
hands and looked through the Shakers spinning around her straight
at Heather just as the Shaker man had earlier. Not with judgment
as he had, but with love mingled with sadness as though she might
be divining sorrow coming. But Heather didn't know if the sadness was for herself or for Heather or even maybe a reflection of
Heather's sorrow for her mother.

Letting her shoulders droop then, Sophrena leaned forward
and shook her arms in a copy of the motion of those around her.
Then she twirled, but slowly and with none of the frantic joy in
the movement that some others were showing as they spun around
like giant tops.

Heather pushed up off the bench. She did not belong here. She
had no choice but to stay in the village until Gideon came home
from the war, but it was not right for her to be here in their meeting. Better for her to find a quiet spot and fill the hour with earnest
prayers. It was not her place to be judging the manner of their
worship. That was between them and the Lord. Nor did she need
a Shaker man telling her to forgive. Her mother's words echoed
through her head often enough with that message.

Before she went out the door, she looked back at Sophrena
once more standing stiffly in the midst of the motion around her.
On her face was that same mingled look of sadness and love she

had given Heather moments before. Something about her looked so very alone that Heather wanted to thread her way through the dancers to wrap her arms around her. But she did not. Instead she went out the door and down the steps away from the building.

She was the one who didn't belong. Not Sophrena.

20

The ice storm rid Gideon of the last of his fantasies about winter in the south. The ice-coated trees groaned like old men when the slightest wind pushed through them. At times a loud crack gave warning of a branch or even a whole tree coming down. The only safe place was inside a building. The tents were no shelter. Most were flattened by the storm, but at least Gideon's hadn't ripped under the weight of the ice.

The next day the sun came out and turned the world into a sparkling wonderland that crunched underfoot with every step. By Monday the ice was gone, but the cold air lingered. Snowflakes floated in the air and stuck tight wherever they landed.

"Better than ice," Jake assured Gideon as he dropped an armload of misshapen tree limbs by the fire. "Leastways we can keep a fire with all the branches brought down by the ice."

"Good in everything," Gideon muttered with no good feelings at all. "Except wet as it is, it's as apt to put out the fire as keep it burning."

"I see you're in fine humor." Jake twisted his mouth to keep

139

from smiling. "So I'm guessing no word from your pretty washer-woman?"

"Not a word. You'd think she could write to me." Gideon scowled at the fire.

"Could be she has. The girl seemed fair struck on you. Why, one could never guess." Jake no longer bothered hiding his smile. "Her sweet words of love are no doubt on their way to you."

"Maybe she's forgotten all about me." Gideon squatted down by the fire and let his head droop down.

"I doubt there's much chance of that with her carrying evidence of your loving." Jake gave Gideon's shoulder a shake. "The mail's just stuck on the other side of the river. They're saying the boats are afraid to come down to Nashville. Not with the Johnny Rebs as thick as fleas on a dog around here."

Gideon threw one of the branches on the fire. The flames disappeared in an explosion of smoke billowing up from the fire.

"Whew." Jake coughed and waved the smoke away from his face. "What are you trying to do? Send her smoke signals?"

Gideon ignored Jake and the smoke. Breathing smoke was part of being in camp. He stared at the flames flickering back to life around the damp wood. "You think we'll be stuck here all winter waiting for fighting weather to come back in the spring?"

"I wouldn't mind that so much. We've wintered in worse places, but I'm thinking we'll be marching out against them before the week's out."

"You said that last week."

"I didn't count on an ice storm. Nor did Pap Thomas, but he'll have us moving soon."

"I just want it to be over. All of it. Done and through."

"Don't we all, lad. Don't we all."

Heather put aside the letter she was writing to Gideon. She'd written one every day and Sophrena had posted them for her, but she'd heard not a word in return. If only she could hear from him to know he was all right. There'd been no news of battles. Sherman was continuing his march to the sea with little opposition from all reports, but Gideon wasn't with him. Gideon was in Nashville where the opposition was gathering, according to the news the Shaker doctor shared with her when he came by on his visits.

The Shakers didn't ignore the happenings in the world. Sophrena said the news was read aloud in the family meetings. Meetings that Sophrena was missing because of Heather. Perhaps another reason for the sadness Heather had glimpsed on her face at their Sunday meeting.

Heather had tried to ask her about it, but each time Sophrena deflected her questions with words of denial.

"The dances can appear strange to those who have never seen them," she'd said when she came back to the cabin after the meeting.

"I feared my presence might be a hindrance to your spirit," Heather said.

"Nay, it is not you who hinders me." She had turned away to bustle about setting out their meal. Bread and meat and applesauce. Cold foods that needed little preparation on the Sabbath.

Now Heather pushed up from her chair to stand by the fire.

Sophrena looked up from her sewing. "Are you all right?" She asked the same question a dozen times a day.

Heather sighed and stared down at the fire. "I am fine. My back aches and I can't seem to take a deep breath any longer and my feet are puffy, but Brother Kenton says all that is to be expected."

"So he did," Sophrena agreed. "That does not make such problems any easier to bear. Perhaps you should lie down."

"I don't want to lie down," Heather said. "I just want it to be over."

Sophrena put aside her sewing and came to rub Heather's back. "It will be soon. Brother Kenton says that babies are very insistent on coming when it is their time. Even the Christ child."

"My young brother wanted me to have a Christmas baby," Heather said, smiling at the thought. Mary too must have felt burdened with the weight of her baby. And to think she'd had to ride a donkey all the day before the Christ was born. Then to end up in a stable.

Here Heather was with a fine roof over her head. A fire to keep her warm. A concerned woman beside her. She had no right to complain. She put her hands on the small of her back and stretched a bit. But then Mary had Joseph with her. While they had shared none of the normal marital relations, Heather imagined that he had cared for Mary with great tenderness. How could he do otherwise after the Lord sent him a dream to reveal the miracle of love growing within his intended bride?

Gideon would be treating her with the same kind of tenderness if he could be here with her. Perhaps a stable would be enough then.

Wednesday night, the captain told Gideon and the rest of his company to be ready come morning. The battle plan had been prepared. The general would relay the orders to the officers and they would move against the Rebels at last.

Gideon slept in his shoes with his hand on his gun. A man needed to be ready. If only he had a letter from Heather to carry in the pocket over his heart. And what of her? Had she gotten his letter of love? He counted up the days since she'd left. It should be almost her time. She could be going into battle herself. A different type of battle to be sure, but one that might be as treacherous.

Gideon wished he was better at praying as he waited for the dawn and the battle to commence. He needed the Lord to watch over his Heather Lou.

The first twinges of something different woke Heather in the early morning hours on Thursday. She lay still and stared up at the darkness. Perhaps it was nothing more than the heaviness of the baby pulling at her back. But she had to bite her lip to keep from groaning and waking Sophrena. No need disturbing her sleep. Not yet. First she would see if there was any rhythm to her pains.

She had almost dozed off again when a new pain jerked her back awake. A similar pain. And suddenly she was afraid. She breathed in and out slowly. If it was time, then it was time. Her mother had never seemed afraid. Weary. Resigned to the pain to come, but not fearful. But then the births she'd witnessed were her mother's fourth and fifth confinements. The first would have been different. The first would always be different. The unknown mixed with anticipation. Pain and joy combined.

Another pain pushed through her. Nothing she couldn't bear. Just something that prodded her into a keen awareness of her body. A signal.

Had Mary the mother of Jesus felt such pains? Or had the Lord's birth been as miraculous as his conception? The Bible said he was delivered of woman, so perhaps Mary had labored to give birth the same as any other mother bearing a child.

Yea, though I walk through the valley of the shadow of death, I will fear no evil.

That was the first thing Mrs. Saunders had done after Heather's father fetched her to help with the birth. Knelt next to the bed and gripped Heather's mother's hands as she spoke that psalm and prayed for a safe journey through that valley for mother and child.

Heather whispered the psalm as she waited for the next pain.

Gideon lined up with his company before dawn. The air was thick with fog. Not the best time to march out against the enemy, but the fog would lift. This way they could get close before the enemy knew they were coming.

"A good thing," the captain said before the signal came to march out of camp. "A blessing of the Lord on our battle plan. Soldiers, we can settle things here and now this very day. Send those Johnny Rebs scurrying back to their rabbit holes down south."

The captain's words came through the fog clear and strong to Gideon's ears, but he was too far back in the ranks to see more than shadowy shapes up where the captain was standing.

Jake had pulled him back as they lined up. "No need being first," he'd whispered. "Give somebody else a turn to be the hero."

Now they stood ready, their guns loaded, the attack planned. Their feet ready to march out wherever the officers pointed them. The captain went on. "So send up your prayers, boys, but step lightly with your mouths shut. No need letting them hear us coming. Leastways till we're in firing range. Then we can wake them up right and proper."

They marched out through the thick fog, trusting the captain to know the right direction.

"You praying, Jake?" Gideon whispered over toward the man beside him.

"That I am, lad, for the both of us. And the Johnny Rebs too."

"The Rebs?" Gideon looked over at him. His face was gray and fuzzy with the blanket of fog between them.

"That they'll take one look at us and skedaddle south." He kept his eyes forward and his words low so Gideon barely heard them right next to him.

"Not likely."

Jake shot a grin over at Gideon. "Who says prayers have to ask for likely things? Our Lord is a powerful God able to do mighty and wondrous things."

"But those on the other side are probably praying too."

"True enough. We'll just have to let the good Lord sort through and find the right answers for us all. Now quit talking and go to praying before the captain shoots us both."

Gideon turned his eyes back to the front and a prayer rose up inside him. Not for the coming battle. *Watch over my Heather Lou.* She'd been hovering in his thoughts since the first moment he'd opened his eyes that morning. *And take me back to her, please, Lord, is my prayer.*

Behind him, one of the soldiers, Gideon didn't know which one, began softly speaking the Twenty-Third Psalm. *The Lord is my shepherd.* The words drifted through the fog and settled over the company. *Yea, though I walk through the valley of the shadow of death, I will fear no evil.*

And they kept marching with the sure knowledge that some of them wouldn't march back.

21

Sophrena sat up in bed. The rising bell wasn't ringing. Nor was daylight creeping through the window, but something had pulled her from sleep. She looked toward Heather's bed beside hers and held her own breath as she listened for the girl's breathing.

"I am awake," the girl said and then let out a small gasp.

"Is it time?" Sophrena pushed back her cover and swung her feet to the floor.

"Perhaps," Heather said with a hint of a tremor in her voice.

"It's still two weeks until Christmas." Sophrena moved across the short space between the beds. "You said Christmas."

"Babies can come early."

"Yea, yea. Of course you are right." Sophrena's heart began beating faster. Heather was having the baby, not her, but even so, her throat felt tight and her hands trembled as she touched the girl's face. "I will get dressed and fetch Brother Kenton."

Heather caught her hand before she could turn away. "No, not yet. The pains are only at the beginning, hardly to be noticed. And while I think they might be the ones to push my baby out into the world, it could be they will fade and amount to nothing. That happened with my mother when she carried little Jimmy. I would not want to disturb Brother Kenton's sleep without reason."

"He said to fetch him at the first signs," Sophrena said, her feet poised to hurry into her shoes and out to the Centre House.

"Not yet," Heather insisted. "Trust me, Aunt Sophrena. It will be better to wait for daylight with just you and me."

Sophrena noted her saying "aunt" instead of "sister." She often made that mistake and each time it touched something in Sophrena's heart. She was to have shaken free of her worldly kin, and for years she had. But now the sound of Heather calling her "aunt" warmed her heart. Perhaps Eldress Lilith was right. Perhaps Heather was pulling her back into worldly ways. She could not deny that she was eager to see the baby Heather carried.

Heather must have noted her hesitation. "You can talk to me and help keep my mind off the pains to come. When the sun is up, you can get the doctor, but now I fear being alone in the dark." She clung to Sophrena's hand.

"If that is what you want." Sophrena held her hand tightly for a moment and then eased free of Heather's grasp. "But let me light a lamp and get dressed so I can build up the fires. If a baby is coming, we need the room to be warm, do we not?"

"We do. And put some water on to boil."

"For washing or tea?" Sophrena asked.

"I don't know. Both perhaps." A smile sounded in Heather's voice. "That's just what dear Mrs. Saunders always told my father to do when my mother was in labor."

"So you were with your mother." That was good. At least one of them would know what to expect.

"I was with the last two. Lucas was fast, slipped out into the world with ease. But not little Jimmy. I feared Mother would die then. He was turned wrong and it took much struggle for him to be born. If not for Mrs. Saunders there with us, I doubt he would have ever drawn breath. She knew what to do."

"We will pray yours will be as your brother Lucas." Sophrena kept her voice even and calm, but Heather's words made her stomach tighten.

Oh dear heavenly Father, she would have no idea what to do. But then the Lord put a calming hand on her. Brother Kenton would know what to do. He had attended births while he was doctoring those of the world. His smile and confident words would be as welcome as the sun come morning.

She stirred awake the coals banked in the fireplace in the bedroom and then lit the lamp. After she pulled on her dress, she smoothed the covers on her bed through long habit. Heather's eyes followed her every movement.

"I'll only be a few moments," she told the girl before she went to build up the fire in the front room and fill the fireplace kettle with water.

Back in the bedroom, she helped Heather up to the invalid potty chair. Sophrena had brought it down from the infirmary after the ice storm. To be ready, she told Heather, in case of more bad weather. She had tried to think of everything. Extra wood in the box. A bucket filled with water. Some biscuits and jam in case the girl got hungry in the night. She could handle those sorts of preparations. What she did not know how to handle were the grimaces of pain that stiffened Heather's body when she helped her stand.

"I didn't think my back would hurt so much," Heather murmured as she leaned heavily on Sophrena. "Maybe it will help if I'm on my feet a few minutes."

But she was eager enough to be back in the bed. Sophrena straightened the covers over her and adjusted her pillow. Then she looked around for more to do, but there was nothing except to wait and watch for the pains to cross the girl's face. She did look so young in the flickering light from the lamp and the fire, not much more than a child herself.

"Sit beside me, Aunt Sophrena." Heather reached a hand toward her. "Talk to me."

Sophrena pulled a straight chair up beside Heather's bed. "What do you want to talk about?" She smoothed down her apron. Her lap felt empty. She thought of the basket of sewing in the other room, but she didn't move to fetch it.

"I don't know. Anything."

"How about names? Have you thought of what you will call your baby?" Sophrena folded her hands in her lap. "What a blessed gift to be able to give a child a name."

"Mary didn't get to pick a name."

"Mary?" Sophrena asked.

"The mother of Jesus." Heather looked toward the ceiling. "The name was given to her."

"Yea, by an angel."

"I've been thinking about her so much. About how she had to make the journey to Bethlehem and found no place to stay except a stable."

"Yea, but the Lord provided."

"He provided for me too." Heather put her hands on her stomach and shut her eyes for a moment. When she opened them again, she reached for Sophrena's hand. "When my father turned me away, the Lord led me here. Where you are. My angel."

"Nay, I cannot compare to an angel," Sophrena said.

"You said you people here want to make your village a heaven on earth. Heaven has angels." Heather smiled. "You could help me find a name for my child. Once we see the baby. Then we will better know a name. Perhaps then a name will whisper down to us from my mother."

"That would be good," Sophrena said.

"Did you never want your own child, Aunt Sophrena?"

"I have loved many young sisters while I have been among the Believers. But my marriage in the world was not a happy one. It's good no child resulted from that union forced on me and on Jerome as well by my father. It was an ill fit for the both of us and a blessing to come among the Shakers and shake free of the sin of it."

"Fathers. They can be so difficult to love." A tear eased out of

Heather's eye and down her cheek. "Will this babe someday think that of his own father? My sweet Gideon?"

"Perhaps not." Sophrena knew no other answer, for who but the Lord could look that far into the future. "Your Gideon may be different. I can see your love for him is strong."

"Mother loved my father just as much and yet he closed the door on me, his child." Heather sighed and brushed at the tears in her eyes. "Did your father close the door on you?"

"My father never seemed to know happiness. My mother suffered from melancholy and he had no patience with her dark moods. He loved his sons, but I was just another female with little use to him. When no boys were attracted to me at the proper time and it appeared I might end up an old maid on his hands forever, he found Jerome. Poor Jerome. He so desired to hold a place of honor in the church, and he thought he needed to be married in order to do so. The Bible speaks of deacons being husband to one wife."

"So he did shove you out of his house and close the door."

"I suppose you could see it that way."

Heather looked back toward the ceiling. Her body tensed for a moment and then she blew out a breath.

"It's almost daylight. Should I go get Brother Kenton now?" Sophrena half rose up out of the chair.

"Not yet." Heather waved her back into the chair. "I will be laboring much of the day, but now I can still talk." She turned her head on the pillow to look straight at Sophrena. "Did you ever see your father again?"

"Nay, I did not. I found a new family here at Harmony Hill." Her words were easy. She had never doubted that choice in those years. Never until this year with her father long dead.

"And so you never forgave him?" Heather looked back up toward the ceiling.

"I shook myself free from him."

"But did you forgive him?" Heather didn't wait for her to answer

151

but went on. "Not caring would not be the same as forgiving, would it?"

"Nay, it would not." Sophrena stared down at her hands and looked inward. A place of bitterness remained there in her heart. Something that shamed her now in the face of this young woman's words.

"This Sacrifice Day the man spoke about at your meeting, when is it?"

"Today is the fifteenth of December. The visitors from the New Lebanon village will come the day before Christmas to lead us in our day of atonement."

"Is that the same as forgiveness?"

"Forgiveness with purpose. One must find a way to make amends for wrongs done, to ask forgiveness from those wronged."

"But what if you are the one wronged?"

"You can't make another feel sorrow for such wrongs, but perhaps we, you and I, can seek forgiveness from the Lord for harboring that injury and forgive our fathers for the wrongs they did to us."

"To do as your Shaker leader said, I'd have to tell my father I forgave him. And then I would have to clear my mind and heart of any memory of the wrong and let it be gone forever."

"That is Sacrifice Day," Sophrena said.

Heather held her hands over her baby again and this time groaned as the pain swept over her.

"The pains are stronger." Sophrena looked toward the window. "The rising bell will ring soon. Let me go get Brother Kenton."

"Not yet." Heather breathed in and out slowly. "First let us have our own Sacrifice Day now, this minute. Mother begged me to forgive my father, knowing that his heart would be hard against me even before I made my way home. I do not want to walk into this valley of the shadow of death with this burden on me. Help me to do as your Shaker brother said."

"We can pray." Sophrena slipped out of the chair onto her knees beside the bed.

"Should I get up to kneel beside you?" Heather tried to get up, but the movement brought a new gasp of pain.

Sophrena pushed her back down. "Nay, the Lord hears our prayers in any position."

"Would you pray the words aloud for me? For both of us? I know you usually pray in silence, but I need the words in my ears today."

"Yea, I will try, though it has been many years since I have spoken a prayer aloud."

"The words are the same unspoken or spoken."

"Yea." Sophrena reached over and took Heather's hands in hers. Then she bent her head and was silent for a long moment. At last she began. "Dear Father in heaven, cleanse our hearts of unforgiving thoughts. Let us forgive as you forgive." She paused again searching for the best words, but there were no best words. Only sincere ones. "I forgive my father for his cold heart toward me. And this child, Heather, she forgives her father for the same."

Heather spoke then. "I forgive my father for closing the door and his heart on me. I will remember his love and forget his anger. Amen."

"Amen," Sophrena echoed her words. She stayed on her knees another long moment, silently asking forgiveness for other sins of the spirit and begging for love and mercy on this mother and her child soon to come into the world.

"Are you still praying?" Heather asked.

"Yea." Sophrena opened her eyes and looked at Heather as the rising bell began to ring. "For you and for your baby."

"Would you pray for Gideon too?"

Sophrena bent her head and prayed for this man she did not know but who she often saw reflected in the love on Heather's face.

When she looked up, Heather said, "Thank you, Aunt Sophre . . ." She didn't finish her word as she stiffened when a new pain grabbed her.

Sophrena scrambled to her feet and held Heather's hands until her breath came easier once more. She smoothed the hair back from the girl's face and had the strongest desire to kiss her forehead like a mother kissing a child's bump to make it better. But this wasn't some little bump or scrape. This was the battle for new life and it had only just begun.

"I am going for Brother Kenton."

The girl caught her sleeve as she started to turn from the bed. "Don't leave me, Aunt Sophrena. I fear being alone."

"But he will know what to do." Sophrena felt so helpless. She knew nothing about birthing babies.

"He will come after the morning meal. He always does. Besides, there is nothing he can do for these pains. It is as it must be. From pain comes joy."

22

By the time the fog began to lift, Gideon's company was in position. The men crouched down behind whatever cover they could find and waited for those in command to give the signal. It was the time Gideon hated the most. That time before the battle began when a man could do nothing but wait. And think about running into enemy fire.

Jake would tell him to stop thinking and start praying. Down the line from him, that would be what Jake was doing. He grabbed onto the Lord any chance he got. Gideon hoped he was praying for him too, because prayer words didn't come easy for Gideon. He was better at coasting along on the prayers of others.

Not that he didn't believe. He did. What man could deny God while standing at the bottom of a hill, knowing men at the top were ready to shoot him? A man like that might be stepping over into eternity at the next sound of gunfire.

As if he'd summoned it, a cannon boom pounded against his ears. Not too close. On another flank of the attack. But a signal of what was to come.

Heather's face rose up in front of his eyes. Back at her home, she was waiting too. For the baby. For him.

The pains grabbed Heather and shook her like a cat grabbing a mouse, squeezing life out of the poor creature, but then when the mouse could bear no more, turning loose to allow it to breathe again. The pains took her into another world. A place where nothing was real except the pain. A wave washing over her and then receding and letting those beside her bed come back into focus.

Dear Sophrena kept dabbing Heather's face with a damp cloth. She looked so frightened that Heather did her best to force a smile out onto her face each time the grip of the pains left her. Brother Kenton was there too. He'd come after the morning meal just as she'd told Sophrena he would. He measured the time between the contractions and smiled with great cheer as he told her everything was as it should be.

He went to see to his other patients even though Sophrena argued against him leaving. He did his best to reassure her. "Babies, especially first babies, are often slow to make their way into the world. I will be back in plenty of time."

"But I won't know what to do." Sophrena's voice had an edge of panic that Heather never thought to hear from her. She always seemed calm and in control, but now she was grasping at the doctor's sleeve to keep him from going.

"Calm yourself, Sister Sophrena. The baby and the mother do all the work. We that are with her simply watch and wait." He patted her hand and bent down to smile directly into Sophrena's face. "I will bring you a calming brew. An herbal tea for the both of you."

He had brought the tea, but whether it calmed Sophrena, Heather couldn't say. It had done nothing for her. But she wasn't nervous, simply becoming very tired. The pains mashed her down into the bed until at times she thought she might be pushed through it to the floor.

Float with the pain. She remembered Mrs. Saunders telling her mother that during her struggle birthing Jimmy. Breathe steady in and out and accept the pain. Don't fight it. Heather tried, but the pain stole her breath until she had to gasp as black closed in around her.

Breathe. She kept hearing that word and she wasn't sure if it was in her mind or if Sophrena was whispering it to her. Breathe. Brother Kenton's voice was there too. Breathe. She could no longer see him smile. She thought others came and went, but she couldn't be sure if she'd really seen them or only imagined them there. All telling her to breathe. Had Joseph told Mary that in the stable that Christmas night or perhaps angels had gathered round her to whisper encouraging words into her ears as the baby Jesus was born?

Heather thought she heard her mother's voice and felt her work-roughened hand grasping hers. She slipped into a gray world of nothing but pain and the need to draw breath. Voices circled in the air above her. Her mother calling her in to supper. Her father reading the Bible on Sundays, his deep voice adding power to the words. Gideon's laugh and whispered words of love. Simon daring her to climb higher. Lucas asking for a Christmas baby. A soldier screaming in the night after a battle. Or maybe that was her screaming while Sophrena and Brother Kenton told her to breathe.

Sophrena didn't know when she'd been more frightened, but she was doing her best to hide it from Heather as she whispered soothing words to her. Words she wasn't sure the girl even heard. Her suffering was worse than anything Sophrena could have imagined.

Brother Kenton said first babies sometimes came hard, but as the hours ticked past, the smile disappeared from his face. He too began to mouth silent prayers as he gently felt Heather's abdomen.

"The baby is turned wrong," he said. "A difficult way to bring a child into the world."

"Can't you do anything?" Sophrena asked.

"Nay," he said, his face grim. "No more than you. Naught but pray."

So they knelt together and prayed. They didn't touch, not as he had touched her in such a natural way earlier as he tried to comfort her distress. Now their distress united them, and their prayers touched and mingled in the air as silently they begged for the Lord's mercy on this mother and child.

At last the order came to charge the Rebel's positions. Gideon scurried from cover to cover and then, when the cover was gone, followed the rest of the troops on toward the Confederate position. A man in front of him fell. Gideon kept going. There was no choice. Not now. Not once the battle commenced. A soldier fired his gun and reloaded. A soldier attacked where the generals pointed. And some soldiers fell.

The Rebels broke and began retreating toward the Granny Smith Turnpike. Gideon and the men around him chased after them. But a retreat didn't always mean the other side was giving up, just falling back to better ground. Bullets kept flying. Cannons continued to belch out their brand of death, with the noise deafening the soldiers to the screams of the injured. Maybe it was better that way. A man couldn't stop to help a friend in the midst of the fighting. He could only promise in his heart to come back after the battle was over—if no bullet found him first.

The sun was sinking. Darkness would end the day's fighting. The captain was motioning the men back. The Confederates had made it to the other side of the pike where they'd be digging in for the battle to commence the next day.

Gideon blew out a long breath of air. He'd made it through another battle. He looked around to see if Jake was still standing too and was relieved to see the big man not far from his side. He smiled, thinking how Jake would tell him he'd loaned him the luck of the Irish or even better, prayed him through yet again.

But the day hadn't ended. Jake let out a yell and ran toward Gideon. Not ten feet away, one of the Rebels was getting to his feet. With the terrible Rebel cry, he fired his gun directly at Gideon, but Jake got there first, his cry as spine chilling as the Rebel's. Gideon crashed to the ground, Jake on top of him. More shots fired, taking down the Rebel, but it was too late for Jake. The bullet had found its mark.

The captain and Gideon carried Jake back to where the company threw up a quick camp. Jake was still breathing, but they feared he wouldn't be for long.

A doctor came, gave him something to dull the pain, and said if he was still alive at daybreak to bring him to the field hospital.

Gideon sat beside him. Drawing breath because of this man, his friend. *No greater love hath any man than to lay down his life for his brother.* Would he have done the same for Jake?

They built a little fire to keep Jake warm. Gideon wet his handkerchief and kept sponging off his friend's face as the man drifted in and out of consciousness. But in the darkest hours of the night, Jake's eyes opened and he stared straight up at Gideon.

"I told you I'd make sure you got home to see that baby."

"You did." Gideon choked back tears and managed a smile. There was no need telling Jake the battle would start up again at daylight. What would he do without Jake?

"Who'd a thought a Johnny Reb would have wanted you dead that bad? He could have waited and crawled off to fight another day. Now we're both dead."

"You're not dead," Gideon said.

"The same as, but don't you worry for me, lad. I've done glimpsed what's ahead and seen my sweet Irene there waiting for me. And she looked to be holding that wee one I lost along with her." A smile slipped across Jake's face before the pain made him wince again.

"Hang in here, Jake. The morning's coming."

"That it is, lad. That it is." A peaceful smile spread across Jake's face. "Love that sweet babe of yours when he comes."

"I'll name him Jacob. After you." Gideon gripped Jake's hand and willed him to keep breathing.

"What if your pretty washerwoman has a girl?" Jake's smile got wider.

"Even then," Gideon promised.

"A girl named Jake." He laughed a little as he closed his eyes. "That would be something. Best say a prayer for a boy."

Jake passed as the first fingers of dawn began to lighten the eastern sky. Gideon covered him with his army blanket and got ready to follow the captain back out to attack the Confederate line. It was what soldiers did.

Sophrena prayed through the night. Brother Kenton stayed with them, doing his best to ease Heather's pain with potions he dribbled down her throat. The girl hardly seemed aware of anything around her and often cried out for her mother.

Eldress Corinne came and prayed over her. She left to gather some of the Believers for more prayer. Eldress Lilith came too, stood over Heather, and watched her desperate struggle. "Her sin must have been great to be so punished."

Sophrena pulled in a breath. "She is little more than a child who fell in love the worldly way. Brother Kenton says the baby is large and turned wrong." Brother Kenton had gone for more herbal potions.

"Yea, the marital union can bring much sorrow."

"You shouldn't speak so where she can hear you." Sophrena stood up and stared at the eldress. "If you have no sympathy in your heart for our little sister, then it would have been better for you to stay away."

"Worldly thoughts are leading you into sin, my sister. I only speak the truth as Mother Ann would." Eldress Lilith's eyes narrowed on Sophrena. "You will have much to ask forgiveness for on Sacrifice Day."

"I will not be the only one who stands in need of forgiveness." Sophrena met her eyes without flinching.

The eldress jabbed a finger toward Sophrena. "I will expect your confession on the morrow."

"Yea, I will have much to confess." Sophrena turned away from the eldress back to Heather. She had no time for the woman's words. Not now. Not with Heather needing her every thought and prayer.

At last those prayers were answered. Brother Kenton brought Sister Doreen back to the cabin with him. "She knows about babies," he said.

"That I do," Sister Doreen said matter-of-factly. "Helped many a baby make his way into the world. Including nine of my own. I know the words to talk her through this and the ways to make it easier."

At her instructions, they elevated the head of the bed to let the natural pull of the earth help. Then she pushed Heather's knees up to make a tent of the sheet over her. "Brother Kenton, you be ready to assist the baby. It could be he will need air very quickly. You hold her hands, Sister Sophrena, and send her as much strength as you possibly can. I am going to be doing the same."

She leaned over close to Heather's ear and began talking so softly Sophrena could only catch a word now and again, but as if by some prayerful miracle, Heather's body visibly relaxed. She began breathing in and out without gasping for air as she had been doing.

Sister Doreen glanced toward Brother Kenton. "Are you ready, Brother? Do you see the baby coming? Remember, you must be quick with your gentle help."

"Maybe you should do it, Sister Doreen," he said.

"Nay, you are skilled. Simply out of practice." She turned back to Heather. "Now, child, it is time. The Lord is going to help you push this baby out. Do you believe that?"

"Yes." Heather murmured her first understandable words for hours. "The Lord is my shepherd."

"And he loves you. And your baby. Now push, my child. Bring this baby into the world where you can hold him."

She gripped Sophrena's hands so tightly her nails cut into the skin of Sophrena's palms as she pushed.

"Good," Sister Doreen said. "This time scream as you push. It is a natural thing. I will scream with you."

Their screams bounced off the walls, but it was a different scream than those that had escaped Heather earlier. These screams had victory in them.

"He's coming," Brother Kenton said. "One more push and I will bring him into the world."

The first rays of the sun pushed through the window as Brother Kenton shouted. "A boy. You have a boy, Sister Heather. A fine boy."

And then the baby cried. Sophrena had never heard a more beautiful sound. Brother Kenton laid the baby on Heather's stomach as he cut the cord.

"Wrap the child in a towel and bring him to his mother," Sister Doreen ordered.

Brother Kenton handed the baby to Sophrena, who had a towel ready. The joy in the doctor's eyes matched that flooding through Sophrena. As she gently wrapped the towel around the baby, she looked down into his round, wrinkled face, his mouth quivering as he cried, and she loved him at once. There was no sin in this child. This was life.

23

Yea, though I walk through the valley of the shadow of death.
The pain was like a live thing. She tried to float with it, but it became a raging torrent throwing her against rocks and pounding her down under the waves of blackness. It conquered her. Completely. She surrendered to it, and when she did, she stepped beyond her body into a different realm.

Her mother was there, reaching for her. "Am I dying?" The words rose from somewhere deep within her.

"Nay, nay." The voice pulled her back. Not her mother's voice, but one she had to heed.

The voice demanded she turn loose of the pain. Demanded she step back from the void swallowing her and do as the voice said. Demanded that she push her baby out into the world.

A baby's cry came through the pain. Her baby's cry. The shadows had tried to swallow her, but she'd ridden out the pain. She'd come through the journey.

Somebody was sponging off her face. Not Sophrena. Doreen. The little woman was leaning over her, speaking, forcing her to come up out of the waters and speak to her.

"Sister Heather, awake for your child. You have done well. He's a fine boy. Sister Sophrena brings him to you."

Heather tried to moisten her lips, but her mouth was too dry. Doreen held a moist cloth to her lips. "Easy, child. The worst is over. You must keep breathing and heal. The joy's begun."

"Joy." Heather managed to get that word out. She forced open her eyes.

Sophrena was there over her, holding a bundle with the dark crown of a tiny head peeking out of the blanket. She placed the baby in the crook of Heather's arm with tears streaming down her cheeks, but her face was glowing.

"Praise God!" Sophrena said softly. "He's so very beautiful."

Behind Sophrena, the doctor was smiling as he said, "A fine boy, Sister Heather. A fine boy."

And he was. Fine. Beautiful. Heather peered down into the red face of her baby and love melted her heart. She peeled the blanket back away from his chin and he pushed out his tiny hand, fingers spread wide as he continued to cry, mouth wide open, small tongue quivering with his distress.

"Shh, little one," she crooned. "You are here. Safe with us." She stroked his cheek in a gentle caress. Her baby. Gideon's baby.

He blinked and his crying stopped with her touch, and somehow new love flowed into a heart she thought had no room for more.

Had Mary felt the same looking down at the Christ child all those years ago? She had known her child was a miracle. She had spoken to angels and yet that first moment of looking at her baby, did she see only the miracle of a child she'd loved at his first quickening in her womb? Did all mothers feel the same? Each child a miracle after their trip through the valley of the shadow of death into a world of light and air. A world that might demand much from them.

As Mary surely hadn't foreseen the path her son would have to travel, Heather could not know the future of this, her child she held. All she could hold onto was the moment.

The moment was good. If only Gideon were there beside her to peer down at this result of their love.

A part of Gideon stayed behind when he marched out at daylight with his company to finish what darkness had halted. Jake was not with him. Jake had always been with him, from the first battle. His prayers had run along beside them. His good humor had kept the grimness of death at bay. His sureness that they'd survive another charge, another hill, had given Gideon courage. And he had survived the charge, would have survived the day, but instead he'd made sure Gideon had been the one to live to see a new sunrise. To someday go home to claim his wife and baby.

But that was yesterday. Only the Lord knew what would happen on this day of battle. Gideon's feet were leaden as he followed Captain Hopkins toward the Rebels.

They would be dug in on the best ground possible. A soldier didn't sleep when the enemy was coming after them. A soldier tried to get ready no matter which side that soldier was fighting on. Gideon wanted to be ready too for whatever was to come, but he was weary of battle.

The morning was spent before the generals had the troops in place. More time for the Rebels to dig in, but a proper battle took planning. General Thomas was not one to rush in unprepared and then have to rally his troops in a retreat. He wanted them to be in the best place to win the day. In front of them was another hill. Would the South never run out of hills?

Every hill and ridge with a name. Tunnel Hill on Missionary Ridge. Cemetery Hill. Culp's Hill at Gettysburg. Dead littered the hills. And now the captain said they had to take Overton Hill, the ground rising in front of them. Each hill had to be conquered. In inches. In blood. Without Jake's prayers.

Heather would be praying for him. She'd have her whole church praying for him. At least those who didn't have Southern sympathies. That might not be many. Her brother Simon had gone south to fight. Two of Gideon's cousins had gone with Simon. Heather's father had forbidden her to go with Gideon, but she had chosen Gideon over her father.

Like the shadow of a bird, worry passed over him. He shook it away. No matter how much he hated Gideon, her father wouldn't deny his own child a safe place. Her mother had told her to follow her heart. Heather would be all right. She had to be all right. He couldn't bear charging up another hill into enemy fire if he couldn't believe that.

The hill waited. He'd rename it. Jake's Hill.

Then take my prayers up it. He heard Jake's voice as clearly as if he were still marching beside him. Gideon stared at the hill in front of him and then squeezed his eyes shut.

"Dear God." That seemed a good start, but then no other prayer words came. Finally he opened his eyes and looked up. "Whatever Jake would have said," he whispered under his breath. "For me and for my Heather Lou."

A strange feeling came over him for a few seconds, then it was as if Jake stood beside him. Smiling. Ready to conquer one more hill.

He could do it. For Heather Lou and a baby named Jake. He would have to write Heather as soon as this battle was over to tell her the name. Boy or girl. She'd understand.

They hadn't talked about names. He'd thought to leave that to her, but not now. Gideon thought of Heather's mother's name. Susan. Susan Jake. Or his mother's name, Frona. Frona Jake. He almost smiled at the thought of either of those combinations. Jake was right. He'd best pray for a boy.

Gunfire sounded and then the noise of artillery pounded into his ears. Not here on this hill yet. On some other hill. The hills around Nashville seemed to have no end. Gideon and his company were still waiting. Sometimes Gideon wondered about the officers who led men into place and then had them wait. Had they never been the man with his feet on the ground and his courage slipping with every moment that passed? Perhaps not. Perhaps that's what made a general. A man who could wait without fear reaching up to grab his throat.

Gideon had no desire to be a general. He didn't even want to be a soldier. Even so, he was one and he would follow orders and charge up yet one more hill. But all he wanted was to still be standing when the guns stopped firing and the war was won. At long last Captain Hopkins gave the signal. No more time for thinking. No more time to worry about the right prayer words. Nothing to do but chase after his captain up the hill, borrowing his courage that never seemed lacking even in the face of artillery fire.

A shout exploded out of Gideon as he ran. "For Jake!"

Men around him picked up the cry until Jake's name was bouncing all over the hill.

The Rebels had dug in, but in their hurry they'd picked positions too close to the rim. They had the high ground but lacked a good angle to shoot down at the charging troops. Still men fell. The soldier to his side screamed and went down. Even with that scream in his ears, it was a shock when the shell slammed into Gideon.

The impact knocked him to his knees. No pain at first. Only disbelief. He felt his shoulder and stared at the red on his hand as though it was somehow betraying him. The blood couldn't be his.

He tried to pick up his gun, but his arm wouldn't move to his bidding. The pain came then, a crushing wave of not only physical pain but the fear that he would be joining Jake in the great beyond. Anger surged through him to burn away the pain. He would make the enemy pay. He grabbed up his gun with his other hand and tried to rise to his feet, but his head was spinning. The noise of battle was all around him, but he was in the shadow of death.

Yea, though I walk through the valley of the shadow of death.

He staggered on up the hill. Captain Hopkins looked back and yelled. Gideon couldn't make out the words as other soldiers pushed past him. He couldn't keep up. He sank to his knees and let them run on. He lay there, feeling his life drain out of him, but then it was as if Jake reached back from heaven to give Gideon a shake. Demand he live.

He began creeping toward the bottom of the hill. For him the war was over, but that didn't mean his life was over. Jake had died to let him see his Heather Lou again. To see his baby. There were medics. His leg was not shot. Only his arm. A man could live without an arm if that had to be.

He left the sounds of battle behind and made his way back to the surgeons.

24

The baby whimpered in the basket Sister Doreen had padded with soft blankets. Sophrena sent up yet another prayer of thanksgiving for Sister Doreen and her midwifery skills. A blessing. A gift. Perhaps the very reason Heather was resting peacefully in the bed in the next room. Brother Kenton had helped to be sure, but it was Sister Doreen who had brought the miracle of birth to pass before it was too late for mother and child.

And what a miracle. Sophrena laid aside her sewing and gently lifted the baby from his basket. He hushed his fussing at once. A week had passed since he had come into the world. A week of rocking and breathing in his baby scent. Seven days without leaving Heather or the baby's side. Other sisters brought their meals. She had not even gone to make confession to Eldress Lilith. A lacking the eldress had come to the cabin to point out to Sophrena.

"Your feet are on a slippery path, Sister Sophrena. I worry for your proper spirit."

"Yea, Eldress, it must seem so to you, but I have been faithful in my prayers. I feel the Lord has not left me."

"Perhaps not, but we must do our part in keeping our hearts pure.

Sacrifice Day will soon be here with visitors from New Lebanon to guide our prayers and spirit renewal." The eldress studied Sophrena a long moment. "We must be spiritually ready in order to properly celebrate the gift of the Christ child." She looked from Sophrena toward the door into the sleeping room where Heather was nursing her baby, but she made no motion to go see them. "Remember, your wrongs must be cleansed by confession and atonements made upon that day."

"Yea," Sophrena answered as meekly as she could.

"May your list of wrongs not get overly long, my sister." A frown creased Eldress Lilith's brow before she went back out the cabin door into the cold December air.

The moment the door closed behind her, Sophrena forgot her. Even now with Sacrifice Day on the morrow, the eldress and her demands didn't seem that important.

The baby consumed Sophrena. Her heart expanded at every blink of his eyes. She felt blessed to be able to care for him and for his mother. At first Heather barely had strength to sit propped up to nurse the baby. Sister Doreen had fashioned pillows to support the child and Brother Kenton mixed tonics to renew the girl's blood.

Ah, Brother Kenton. A change had come between them. A change had come over Sophrena. Brother Kenton was the same. A cheerful brother. The moment of joy they had shared at the first mewling cry of the newborn baby had seared through Sophrena and altered something in her heart.

Sophrena crooned at the little person in her arms and marveled at his completeness. She had given him his first bath, examining him from head to toe, as had Brother Kenton.

The babe had no name yet. Heather wanted to wait until his father saw him before she spoke his name. A letter had come from her Gideon that she read over and over. Even now, Sophrena was sure it was under her pillow or tucked into the bodice of her dress. She might wear the Shaker dress, but she had not the Shaker heart.

Sophrena held the baby up to her shoulder and put her lips to his soft cheek. A memory of doing the same years before with Heather's mother when she was a baby came to her. She had been only eight years older than Susan, but that was old enough to be allowed some of the baby's care. Her first and only time with a baby until now. Dear Susan, who would never get to hold this child of her child. Had the Lord allowed her, Sophrena, to step into Susan's shoes for this time? Was it God's plan? Was her Shaker dress merely covering over a heart that had turned worldly?

The baby didn't look like Gideon. The baby didn't look like her. It was Lucas she saw when she peered down into his face. Sweet child, Lucas, who had wanted her to have a Christmas baby. Lucas who looked so like his father. Like her father.

Beth had written her again. Had sent her Gideon's letter. The letter had been written days ago, but he'd been alive then. Loving her. Missing her.

Heather had the letter memorized but that didn't keep her from unfolding it and feasting her eyes on the words formed by Gideon's hand. Words from his heart.

Beth assured Heather of her father's softening heart too. Heather didn't know if she could believe that, but he had not destroyed Gideon's letter. He had let Beth send it to her.

The Shaker Sacrifice Day was coming. On that day, she intended to write her father a letter of forgiveness. She and Sophrena had prayed for such forgiveness of their fathers in the early hours of her labor, but written words would make it complete.

Now she could only think of Gideon's baby. She had not decided on his name. Perhaps Gideon for his father. But she remembered Simon and Jimmy and so she delayed declaring a name. The Shakers who brought gifts and peered down at him simply called him "little brother." That made Heather smile. It was as if she had brought them a special gift for the Christmas season. A baby to remind them of the Christ child. Perhaps she would decide on a name Christmas Day. A gift to her and to her baby.

She was no longer waiting for the baby, but still she waited. For Gideon. For her strength to return. For a name. For God's plan as to what next. Had Mary felt the same? She had a name for her child given to her by an angel. Had she hoped she and Joseph could settle in Nazareth close to her family and see their son grow and be joined by other babies come in the more natural way? Had she, like Heather, simply wanted things to be normal? Then Joseph had the dream to flee to Egypt. Not her plan, but God's plan.

That was Heather's prayer now. That God would show her a plan. That he would send Gideon home. That prayer circled round and round the way the Shaker sisters had whirled in their meeting. And so she waited in the midst of the Shakers for what might happen next. For the Shaker Sacrifice Day. For Christmas. For Gideon. For God's plan.

Gideon drifted up out of the darkness pulled by the voice of a doctor. Pain had accompanied his journey through a valley of darkness, but there in the darkest moment, he'd seen his Heather Lou smiling at him, beckoning to him, her eyes alight with joy. She held a bundle in the crook of her arm. His baby. He couldn't see him, but he knew.

Then Jake was there too, but not like Heather. Not ahead. He was right beside Gideon, prodding him back to life no matter the pain.

He was in a church. The pews were all pushed to the side to make room for the makeshift pallets for the wounded. He tried to judge how badly he was hurt. Somebody let out a scream across the room. Gideon wasn't that bad. He wasn't weeping. He wasn't dying.

But he was hurt. He peeked over at the bandages to see red oozing through. Not a good thing, but at least he was alive and not feverish. He could stand. He could walk. As soon as the doctors knew that, they ordered him gone from the hospital in the church so a more severely wounded man could be brought in to the shelter.

"Where to, sir? My company chased after the Rebels, I'm told." Gideon looked at the the officer behind a table outside the makeshift hospital and waited for his orders.

"Where would you like to go, soldier?"

"Home, sir." Gideon looked beyond the officer's head toward the north.

"How far is home?" The officer looked up at him from the papers he was shuffling.

"Kentucky, sir. My wife returned there to have our baby." Gideon bit the inside of his lip and concentrated on not weaving back and forth on his feet in spite of the way his head was spinning. "She was a washerwoman with our unit before we came south."

The officer gave him a closer look. "I remember her. Pretty girl. Always with a ready smile even with all those washtubs to tend."

"Yes sir. That was my Heather Lou."

"You're a fortunate man, soldier."

"Yes sir. I'm still breathing."

"That you are, but your gun-toting arm appears disabled." The man scribbled something on a piece of paper and handed it to Gideon. "You're out of the army, soldier. Medical reasons."

Gideon took the paper as though it were gold. "Thank you, sir."

"You can be proud, soldier. We chased those Rebels back into their rabbit holes. Hood's Tennessee army is finished. Pap Thomas knows how to win the day." The officer stood up and shook Gideon's left hand. "Go see if that baby's born yet."

It hadn't been easy. Not for a Union soldier in territory that might be controlled by the North but was South. Yet he found a way. The nearness of Christmas must have softened people's hearts no matter the uniform. A farmer gave him a ragged coat when he noted him shivering on the wagon seat beside him. Tattered and none too clean but warm. Another shared his bread and cheese. Somehow, blessing by blessing as the days passed, he made it north, by boat, by train, by wagon. He tried not to think about his wound even though the pain was sometimes intense during the jarring journey. At the end of that journey would be his Heather Lou.

25

Sacrifice Day dawned clear and cold. Not even one cloud marred the deep blue of sky. A day with nothing hidden. Sophrena had paused a moment to accept that thought as she hurried to the privy. She didn't like leaving Heather alone even though the girl was recovering quickly. She refused to lie abed and had even joined in with Sophrena's sewing again whenever the baby slept.

When Sophrena went back into the cabin, Heather had moved close to the fire in the sleeping room. The girl was often chilled, but Brother Kenton said that was only natural after the blood she'd lost while birthing her child.

Brother Kenton hadn't been to the cabin for three days. That was proof of Heather's improved health. Sister Doreen came often, coaching Heather on her mother duties and helping Sophrena know what care was needed for both mother and child. Other sisters brought small gifts. A newly sewn gown or blanket. A knitted cap. A soft bib. A whistle carved by Brother Josiah. Sophrena had seen him place it on the step and then run away as if the very devil were after him.

"The Lord has gifted us with a fine day for our Sacrifice Day," Sophrena said as she put another chunk of wood on the fire.

Heather held her hands out toward the flames. "Why do they call it Sacrifice Day?"

Sophrena looked up from sweeping the ashes back into the fireplace. "It is a day of prayer when hearts must be searched and sacrifices of self made."

"I thought you told me it was a day to forgive. To make amends." She sat down in the chair by the fireplace.

When the baby began to whimper, Sophrena brushed off her hands and lifted him from his warm nest on the bed. He was growing. Already looking different as he waved his little fists in the air. Perhaps in protest of being left alone. Perhaps just to be noticed. He hushed his whimpers as soon as Sophrena picked him up, and the flicker of a smile passed across his face.

She handed him to Heather. She watched her adjust her dress to nurse the baby before she answered her. "Think, Sister Heather, of how it is the same. Forgiveness requires a sacrifice of pride. A humbling of the spirit. An increase of selfless love. A time when you allow others' feelings to be more important than your own."

"I am going to write my father of my forgiveness." Heather kept her eyes on the nursing baby and ran her finger around this cheek. "His father is going to love him so much."

"Yea." Sophrena agreed. Who could not love this precious child? She told herself she should be cleaning, readying the house and her heart for the day, but instead she stood idle and watched the mother and child.

Heather looked up at her. "Will he one day have reason to forgive his father as I had need to forgive mine?"

"The future can only be known by God."

"I dreamed of Gideon." Heather's eyes settled back on the baby. "He was calling to me."

"What did he call?"

"I don't know. The words were swallowed by the dream."

"But I sense it, the dream, made you uneasy." Sophrena stepped over to the girl's chair and touched her shoulder.

"It did not seem happy."

"You have been worried about him after Brother Kenton brought news of the Union victory at Nashville. It is only natural that those worries appear in your dreams."

"What would I do without you, dear Aunt Sophrena?" Heather leaned her head over to touch her cheek to Sophrena's hand.

Sophrena dropped a kiss down on top of her head before she took the broom from its hook again. A house should be free of dirt on Sacrifice Day.

Heather turned her attention back to her baby as she shifted him to her other breast. After a moment, she looked over at Sophrena. "Have you anyone to forgive on this day?"

"More to ask forgiveness."

"Are you talking about that Eldress Lilith?" Heather didn't wait for Sophrena to answer. "I wouldn't ask her for anything. She needs a more charitable heart."

Sophrena smiled as she sat the broom aside to straighten the bed covers. "But that is why there is need for much prayer and contemplation on Sacrifice Day."

Heather breathed out a sigh. "Another reason I could never be a Shaker."

"You pray." Sophrena scooted the bed to the side in order to sweep away any dust hiding under it.

"But not for the same things you pray for." Heather kept her eyes on her baby. "I pray for my baby. I pray for his father. I pray for you."

Sophrena hung the broom back up and sat down in the chair by the girl. "What do you pray for me?"

"You may not want to hear it," Heather said without looking up.

"Nay, I will not be upset by whatever you say. I know you are of the world."

"That is what I pray for you, dear Aunt Sophrena." Heather

177

cradled her baby gently against her and reached across the space between their chairs to touch Sophrena's hand. "That you will come away from here and be part of our family again. That you will know love as I do."

"I am too old for such love even if I were not a Shaker."

"Are you so sure?" Heather looked back down at her baby and hesitated before she spoke again. "I have seen the way you look at Brother Kenton."

Sophrena shifted her eyes away from Heather and stared at the fire. She breathed in and out slowly. "Such feelings destroy the peace we strive for here at Harmony Hill."

"Denying the feelings does not bring peace to your heart, does it?" Heather looked up at her.

"Nay. But I have been a Shaker for many years. I cannot imagine another life."

"I don't believe that. You have lived another life with me here in this cabin since I came. You hold my baby with great love and tenderness. And even before that, you reached out to my mother with your letters."

"I did."

"Mother wrote me a letter before she passed. She thought perhaps God stirred your heart to write her because he knew the hard times coming for us. That this was his plan, and then when I came into your village, you echoed her words." Heather put the baby up to her shoulder and rubbed his back to help him burp. "God's plan. Perhaps God is giving you a new plan on this Sacrifice Day."

"Eldress Lilith says not." Sophrena kept her eyes on the fire.

"It is not Eldress Lilith's plan you have to ponder on this day. It is God's plan. For you." Heather's voice was soft but insistent. "Perhaps that is what you need to contemplate on this Sacrifice Day. Should we not listen to God first?"

"And have you done so?" Sophrena asked.

"Not always as I should, but the Lord has blessed me. I have forgiven my father. Now I will pray that my father will forgive me on this day. And I am going to pray that Gideon will see this child, his son."

"Good prayers."

"What will you pray, Aunt Sophrena?"

Sophrena stared at the fire a long moment without moving. She thought of the sisters, Mary and Martha in the Bible. One so busy there was no time for thought of anything but duties to be done. The other contemplating the truths the Lord was sharing with them. Was it not time for her to be like that sister? She looked over at Heather and answered her at last. "I will pray that the Lord reveals my path and that it will be a path I can step upon with joy."

"I will pray the same for you, and that we will both have the courage to embrace the gifts he sends us."

26

The morning before Christmas, Gideon finally topped the hill and looked down at the farmhouse where his Heather Lou would be awaiting him. The last days had been hard with pain grabbing him every time he moved his shoulder. He'd thought about stopping to find a doctor, to get a fresh bandage, but every minute he wasn't moving north was another minute before he could see Heather.

Smoke curled up out of the chimney of her house, inviting him to hurry. He imagined her sitting with her mother around the stove, maybe knitting a baby sweater. It was early in the day. He'd gotten off the train in Danville the evening before and walked until near dark before taking shelter in a barn beside the road. He couldn't sleep. The pain from his shoulder made it impossible to find a comfortable position, but even more, he couldn't sleep because Heather was on his mind. She'd once told him he could sleep anywhere. Hard ground or soft. Cold nights or hot days. With cannons booming or in deep silence. It had been easy to sleep with her hand on his chest, promising her love.

But the night before, his eagerness to see her kept him awake.

She was so near, but he had no choice except to wait for daylight. A stumble in the dark and a fall on his shoulder might be more than he could stand. But once he was with her, once her hands were touching him again, then he would heal.

He looked down at her house. The thought of her face in front of his eyes gave his legs new energy. He called out her name and began to run down the hill.

A boy stepped from the side of the barn to stop him. Heather's little brother. All arms and legs, Willie had grown nearly as tall as Gideon.

"Gideon, is that you?" The boy had no smile of welcome on his face. Instead he looked almost afraid as he took a quick look back over his shoulder toward the barn doors.

"I haven't changed so much that you don't recognize me, have I, Willie?"

"You're not looking too good, but I know you." Willie took another nervous look behind him. He kept his voice low. "But you better get on out of here before Pa sees you."

"I won't be leaving without Heather." Gideon looked past the boy toward the house.

"Heather's not here, and if he sees you, Pa's as apt to shoot you as not." Willie grabbed hold of Gideon's arm and tried to pull him back behind the barn. "He ain't got no use for Yankees."

Gideon didn't let Willie budge him. A sick feeling was rising up inside him. She had to be here. What did he mean she wasn't here? He grabbed Willie's jacket. "Where is she?"

"Let go of my boy!" Heather's father stepped out of the barn and leveled a rifle at Gideon.

Willie jerked free from Gideon, but instead of moving away, the boy put himself between his father and Gideon. "He was just leaving, Pa."

"Don't waste your pity on a Yankee." The man's voice was full of contempt. "Step aside, Son. Now."

Willie did as his father ordered. His eyes flashed from Gideon to his father's face and back again before, without a word, he took off for the house, running as if his life depended on it. Mr. Thornton didn't let his eyes waver from Gideon as he kept the gun leveled on him.

Gideon stared back at him. "Where is she?"

"Gone. They're all gone." The gun wobbled a bit, but then the man pulled it back up straight.

Gideon hardly noticed it. He could think of nothing but where Heather might be. "She can't be gone. She has to be here."

"Gone, I said." His voice was rough. "The same as Simon felled at Gettysburg and her mother and Jimmy lost to the cholera. All gone. The Lord giveth and the Lord taketh away."

"Gone? You can't mean my Heather Lou is dead." He couldn't bear the thought.

"She was dead to me the day she went off with a Yankee."

"But she was carrying my child." Despair mashed him down until it was all he could do to stay on his feet. Behind the man, he could see Willie and Heather's sister, Beth, running toward them. The little brother, Lucas, trailed after her, wailing as he tried to keep up.

"Pa," she screamed. "No."

He paid her no mind as he stared at Gideon. "What do I care about your child?" But a flash of pain in his eyes gave lie to his words. "I told her not to go with you."

"But she came home to have him. Here where she felt safe and loved."

"I sent her away. She had no place here." He kept his jaw clenched, but the timbre of regret was in his words.

"Where?"

"What does that matter to you? You'll not live to see another sunrise."

"You can shoot me, but you can never make me quit loving your daughter." He held his arms out beside him, surrendering. It seemed a long way to walk to die when he could have done that on the battlefield.

Beth stopped a few paces away from them as though she feared getting too close. She grabbed at her breath and spoke in a voice that made Gideon think of her mother. "Pa, you can't shoot Heather's husband." When he didn't so much as look sideways at her, she went on. "Thou shalt not kill. You taught us the Ten Commandments."

"This is war," he said.

"The war is over for us," she said firmly. "We need no more dying."

"Death comes whether we need it or not." He raised the gun up to his shoulder and sighted down the barrel at Gideon. Willie's eyes popped open bigger and Lucas hid his face in his sister's skirt. Their father paid no notice to them as he asked Gideon, "Is the war over?"

"For me it is." Gideon locked his eyes on Mr. Thornton. "Is it over for you?"

"It's over, Pa," Beth spoke up. "More killing won't bring Simon back."

"Hush, girl," her father ordered. Lucas began wailing louder. "You too, Lucas."

"But Pa, you can't kill him on Christmas," the little boy said between sobs.

"It's not Christmas."

"But Beth says Heather just had a baby. A Christmas baby."

"She's had the baby?" Gideon forgot the gun pointed at him as he stepped toward Beth. "The baby's here?"

"We got a letter yesterday from Aunt Sophrena. You have a boy." Beth smiled at him.

His head began to spin. He had a son. "And Heather?"

"Aunt Sophrena writes she had a difficult confinement but she made it through."

"Yea, though I walk through the valley of the shadow of death," Gideon whispered.

A valley they had both been in during the last weeks. A valley he might still be walking through. He looked around at Heather's father. The man had lowered his gun and was staring away toward a cluster of trees in the distance.

"Surely goodness and mercy shall follow me all the days of my life, and I will dwell in the house of the Lord forever," the man said.

"We read that at Mother's funeral." Beth pushed past Gideon toward her father. Without hesitation, she put an arm around his waist and leaned her head against his shoulder.

"Sometimes I don't think I can keep going without her," he said. "She wasn't supposed to die."

"Too much dying," Beth whispered.

Gideon thought of the bodies lined up after a battle, awaiting burial. Jake's body had been in one of those lines. Now his body might end up in another place awaiting the mercy of burial. But dear God, please let him see Heather one more time. And his baby. He so wanted to see his son. Jake had died to give him that chance.

"Where is she?" he asked.

"The Shaker village in the next county," Willie spoke up. "You might have come right by there."

"And I'm going right back." Gideon turned too quickly toward the road and the combination of too much blood lost and no food since he'd gotten off the train the day before sapped him of energy. He reached for something to hold on to, but there was nothing but the thought of Heather and his baby. Black settled around him and his knees buckled.

Willie came to help him. "He's bleeding."

"Did you shoot him, Pa?" Lucas started wailing again.

Gideon tried to get back to his feet, but even with the thought of Heather waiting for him, he couldn't pull up enough strength to keep going. He'd have to sit there on the ground and rest awhile. And hope the man would pick up his gun and go away without shooting him.

"Stop your caterwauling, Lucas. I didn't shoot him." He handed his gun over to Beth and moved to reach down to Gideon. "Come on, Willie. Let's get him in the house and see to him. Your sister's right. There's been enough dying."

Gideon drifted in and out of consciousness. He was in a warm place. The hands washing his wound were gentle. Strong arms lifted him up and held water to his lips. And then broth. Heather's house. Heather's family. But she wasn't there. He had to get to Heather. To his son. He had to tell her the baby's name.

Finally he was able to push open his eyes and keep them open. He was on a cot. Heather's father was in a chair beside him. The gun was nowhere in sight. Gideon raised his head and swung his feet out on the floor. The man watched him without a word.

Gideon sat there on the edge of the cot to let his head clear before he said, "Thank you for not shooting me."

"Lucas was right," the man said. "Christmas is a bad time for killing."

Gideon looked toward the window. The light was dimming, but he had no idea how long he'd been out. Was it evening or morning? Maybe it was Christmas Day. He licked his lips and said, "Is it Christmas?"

"Susan would say so. She liked the night before the same as the day. Made the children new nightshirts and gowns. Let them sit up till midnight eating popcorn and chocolate candy. Then she had me read about the angels coming to the shepherds before she sent them off to bed." He looked up at the ceiling. "I swear there were nights I could hear those angels singing."

Across the room, Beth and the two boys stood by the fire listening. Gideon could see tears glistening on the girl's cheeks as she reached to pull Lucas closer to her. Nobody said anything as they waited for Mr. Thornton to go on.

He stared down at his hands spread out on his thighs a long moment before he said, "But it was never the angels. It was always Susan, and now I'll never hear that singing again."

Words popped in and out of Gideon's mind, but none seemed right. Finally because the man seemed to be waiting for something from him, he said simply, "She loved you."

"She did. God only knows why, but she did. And I loved her." He raised his eyes to stare at Gideon with challenge. "Do you love my daughter that way?"

"I love her more than life." Gideon managed to get to his feet. "I've got to go find her."

The man stood up and gently shoved him back onto the cot. "The day is almost gone. When Christmas dawns on the morrow, we will go in the wagon. All of us. I hear my Susan telling me to give you that gift."

"It will be a gift to all of us," Beth whispered. "A wonderful Christmas gift to see our sister and her new baby. Thank you, Pa. Mama will be singing a song of joy just for you."

He didn't smile, but a tear slipped out of his eye and slid down his cheek. He didn't brush it away, just blew out a breath of air, and stalked out of the cabin. Willie started to follow him, but Beth stopped him. "Best let him listen for Mama's song alone, Willie. Come, we'll go pop some corn."

Gideon lay back on the pillow and listened to the corn popping. Next Christmas, he and Heather would begin their own special times with little Jake.

27

Sophrena did everything a Believer was supposed to do on Sacrifice Day. She prayed. She confessed. She asked forgiveness. She forgave. Eldress Lilith gave her a blessing. Sister Edna smiled and told her she would be glad when she came back to share the retiring room with her and the other sisters. Brother Kenton looked surprised and then a bit uneasy when she asked his forgiveness for wrong thoughts toward him. She stopped him on the porch as he left the cabin after checking on Heather and the baby.

He stared down at his medicine bag as he seemed to search for the proper words. Finally with a gentle look, he said, "We have shared much in the last few weeks, Sister Sophrena. I have admired your caring spirit and devoted ways to our young sister. Such times of closeness can awaken feelings that tempt us into worldly thinking."

"Yea." Sophrena had already faced the truth that Brother Kenton had not looked upon her with the same affection that had sprung awake in her own heart. That seemed even more reason to ask his forgiveness on Sacrifice Day. "I have struggled with worldly thoughts all through the year."

"Even before Sister Heather came among us?" He let his eyes

touch on Sophrena's face and then quickly slid his gaze back to the ground.

"Yea. Your smile awakened joy within me."

"Then I must ask your forgiveness for setting a worldly temptation in front of you. Such was not my intent. I rejoice in the peaceful love of the brothers and sisters here in our village."

"Much simple joy can be found here. It has been mine for many years."

He looked up at her, this time meeting her eyes. "But now it is no longer?"

"I have entertained feelings I have been unable to whirl away."

"Perhaps I could make you a tonic," he suggested.

"Nay." Sophrena couldn't keep a smile from tugging at her lips. "There are some things for which there are no tonics."

Again he looked uneasy. "I am sorry," he started.

She waved away his words. "Don't be, my brother. My spirit is well. I am forgiven. I am loved. Whatever God's plan for me, joy is alive in my heart."

And it was. She watched him walk away with no sorrow for his leaving. Inside, Heather and the baby awaited her love. Whatever happened on the morrow, she would know it was God's plan.

Heather woke early on Christmas Day. Her spirit felt light in spite of her worry for Gideon. She had emptied her heart of resentment toward her father for refusing to welcome her home. She had forgiven him and prayed on the Shakers' Sacrifice Day that somehow he would know her forgiveness.

The Lord had made good come from his anger at her. She had found this warm place of welcome with Sophrena. Not her mother, but a woman she could love much the same as she did her mother. After their morning meal, Heather caught Sophrena's hand as she got up to clear away their dishes before she left for the Shakers' Christmas Day worship.

"I have no gift for you, Aunt Sophrena. Nothing but the love I feel for you in my heart. You have been a gift to me. An angel supplied by the Lord when I most needed it."

Sophrena put her arms around Heather. "Nay, my child. You are the gift. You and your sweet baby. The Lord noted my weary spirit and sent you to renew my joy. I could have no better gift."

An easy feeling fell over them. The blessing of Christmas love. After Sophrena left for the Shaker worship, Heather held her baby against her shoulder and whispered into his ear. "I will give you never-ending love, my child, just as my mother gave me. Prayers and love."

He burped in answer and Heather laughed. A good feeling to laugh. "And is that a reminder that it is time for me to give you a name?"

From up in the village, the sound of the Shakers' singing drifted down to the cabin. She held the baby close against her and went to open the door in order to hear the sounds of worship better. There was joy in the songs. Sophrena had told her that sometimes they gave one another imaginary gifts at their Christmas worship. Things like baskets of love or ribbons of happiness. That would be the gift she would like to unwrap for Sophrena. Happiness.

Perhaps if she had gone with Sophrena to worship, one of the Shaker sisters or brothers would have given her the gift of the best name for her baby. They had already brought him many good gifts. Tactile things she could touch such as bibs and blankets. But how much more important were those gifts that could not be touched.

Had Mary held the Christ child close to her heart when the wise men came bringing their gifts and thought the same? That her own love and that of Joseph's were better gifts than the gold, frankincense, and myrrh. Then there was the love of God evidenced by a new star in heaven. Surely that was the best gift of all.

God loved her baby too. That was why he had made a way for her. She bent her head and listened to the music of the voices while praying that the Lord was making a way for Gideon.

Sun streamed down on her, but the air was cool. She was turning back inside to settle the baby in his basket when she caught sight of a wagon coming. Dark brown horses with white blazes on their faces like her father's. She froze and stared at the wagon. Could that be her father sitting so straight and unbending on the wagon seat with Willie beside him? Was she only imagining them because her heart so needed family on this Christmas Day?

She hardly dared breathe as the wagon came closer. *God's plan*, a voice whispered in her head. Her mother's voice. Had her father felt her forgiveness? Had that been what drew him here? Pray God it was true.

As they came nearer, there was no doubt it was her father and Willie. The boy was turning to talk to someone in the wagon behind him. Beth stood up and looked toward the cabin. A smile spread across Heather's face at this beautiful gift coming toward her. Then another person was pulling up to stand behind the wagon seat and Heather's heart pounded up into her throat. Gideon.

She shouted his name, and clutching the baby close to her, she rushed to meet the wagon with tears of joy streaming down her cheeks. On the wagon, Beth grabbed Gideon's coat when he started to climb over the side, but he jerked free of her grasp and jumped from the wagon. He staggered and nearly fell, but then he found his feet and began running toward Heather.

He was pale with one arm bandaged against his body, but he wrapped the other around her. "My Heather Lou."

His lips sought hers and Heather sent thanks to the Lord for this Christmas blessing.

The baby was crying and fighting against her. Heather pulled back from Gideon and peeled the blanket away from their baby's face. Gideon stared down at him with wonder plain on his face. "My son. Jacob." He touched the baby's hand and the baby grasped Gideon's finger and hushed crying.

"Jacob." Heather looked from the baby to Gideon. "Have you brought him his name?"

"I hope you haven't already given him another name." Gideon suddenly looked worried. "I did promise Jake and it's a promise I must keep."

She smiled and touched Gideon's cheek. "I'm glad you want to name him after Jake. I love Jake. He's all right, isn't he?"

Gideon looked sad. "He'd tell you that was so, if he could. I watched him die, but he was smiling when he passed over with the morning coming."

"Simon's dead too," Heather said. "And Mother and little Jimmy." She blinked back more tears. These of sorrow for all they had lost.

"I know. Your father told me." He gently brushed away her tears.

"We'll call him Jacob Simon." She looked down at the baby and smiled. "Jacob Simon Worth."

Her father spoke from the wagon where they had all been watching Gideon meet his child. His voice was gruff. "Get my grandson back inside before he catches a chill."

Heather looked up at her father and a laugh bubbled up out of her.

"A chill is no laughing matter." He wasn't exactly smiling, but neither was he frowning.

The Shaker silence fled the small cabin as they gathered around the fire and all tried to talk at once. Gideon sat and held his baby. Then Beth took her turn. Willie was satisfied with a peek and Lucas kissed his forehead and declared him a Christmas baby. Finally, Beth laid the baby in their father's arms.

"Jacob Simon, meet your grandfather," Beth said.

Their father looked down at the baby and then up at Heather. "I was wrong to chase you from my door." There was pain in his face.

"Worry not, Father. I forgave you yesterday." When he looked puzzled, she went on. "The Shakers have a day they call Sacrifice Day when they are to forgive and make atonements for wrongs. So I forgave you. Now I ask you to forgive me in turn for any hurts I caused you and for not being there with Mother when she passed."

193

Silence fell over them all as he looked at her and then at Gideon and finally at the baby. "It is time we were a family again."

Sophrena came through the door in time to hear him. "Family," she echoed. She looked at them in turn, her expression softening on each one as though she were taking them into her heart. Even Gideon. But especially Lucas who watched her with big eyes, seeing the same thing Heather had seen when she first met Sophrena.

Lucas moved toward her as if drawn by an invisible band. "You look like Mama," he said.

Sophrena held out her arms to him and he walked into her embrace. "The gift of family," she said softly as she held the little boy close to her.

Sophrena brought them all food and they ate their Christmas dinner in the cabin. Not silently as she was accustomed to at the Shaker table, but with much talk and much joy. She held the baby and dreaded the meal to be finished, for she knew then they would leave. A family reunited. Gideon and Heather sat touching hands, sharing a special closeness in the midst of the others.

Then the food was eaten, the dishes cleared away. Susan's husband was standing, saying they must return home before darkness caught them. The baby's things were packed. His gowns and blankets. All the little gifts. Sophrena stood by the fire and watched. Her arms had never felt so empty. Her heart never so barren.

They were ready to go. Heather came to her. "Come with us."

"The Lord put me here," she said.

"He did, but now he has opened a new door to you. Come with us, Aunt Sophrena."

"I would have no place there."

"There is always a place for family." Heather looked at Gideon and then her father.

Susan's husband looked straight at Sophrena and spoke without hesitation. "We can build houses in the spring."

They watched her then, waiting. She too was waiting. For what she wasn't sure.

The young boy, Lucas, ran to put his arms around her waist. "You can be my new mother so Beth can get married to Perry."

That made the young girl blush. And Sophrena felt a whirl in her head. God's plan from her first letter reaching out to Susan, to Heather and her baby, and now to this boy who needed her love. A gift. Without a word, she turned and took down her cloak to follow them out the door. Willie helped her up into the wagon filled with hay to soften the bounces. Heather took her hand and kissed it before she settled beside her husband. Lucas and Beth sat down on either side of Sophrena.

Beth took her hand. "You can share my bed, Aunt Sophrena, until we get those houses built."

Susan's husband climbed up on the wagon seat with his son Willie and started the horses moving out of the village. As she passed by the Centre House, Sophrena glimpsed Sister Edna's face in one of the windows. Good. She could tell the others. She lifted her hand in a wave that Sister Edna did not acknowledge. She would not. They would mourn Sophrena's leaving as one who had fallen into sin.

But the Lord had thrown open this door. A gift to her. A gift to be simple. A gift to be free.

As the wagon continued on out of Harmony Hill, Sophrena did not look back.

Acknowledgments

This Shaker Christmas story would have never come about if not for a visit several years ago from my editor, Lonnie Hull DuPont, and my agent, Wendy Lawson. We were getting ready to tour the Pleasant Hill Shaker village near my home when one of them said, "Wouldn't a Shaker Christmas book be fun?" It wasn't the Christmas season, and at the time, I knew nothing about how the Shakers even celebrated Christmas, but I took their challenge. This story is the result, and I thank Lonnie and Wendy for their enthusiasm for the idea and for their continual encouragement.

While the words that tell this story of love and forgiveness are mine, I am grateful to the many hands it has passed through on its way to the lovely package you, the reader, now hold. I appreciate everyone at Revell Books who helped make this book the best it can be.

Christmas is a great time to thank my family for their love and support. Last, but never least, I thank the Lord for the gift of words and for giving me readers like you. Thank you so much and may your every Christmas be blessed.

Song Credits

Page 129—Simple Gifts—Manuscript Hymnals, 1937–47
Page 133—The Union of the Spirit—Anonymous Author; from *Simple Wisdom* by Kathleen Mahoney, published by Penguin Group, 1993

Ann H. Gabhart lives on a farm just over the hill from where she grew up in central Kentucky. She loves books, playing with her grandkids, and walking with her dog. She and her husband are blessed with three children and nine grandchildren.

Ann is the author of more than twenty novels for adults and young adults. Her Shaker novel, *The Outsider*, was a Christian Book Awards finalist in the fiction category. *Angel Sister*, Ann's first Rosey Corner book, was a nominee for inspirational novel of 2011 by *RT Book Reviews* magazine.

Visit Ann's website at www.annhgabhart.com.

Meet ANN H. GABHART at
WWW.ANNHGABHART.COM

Be the First to Learn about New Releases,
Read Her Blog, and Sign Up for Her Newsletter

CONNECT WITH ANN AT

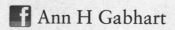 Ann H Gabhart

 AnnHGabhart

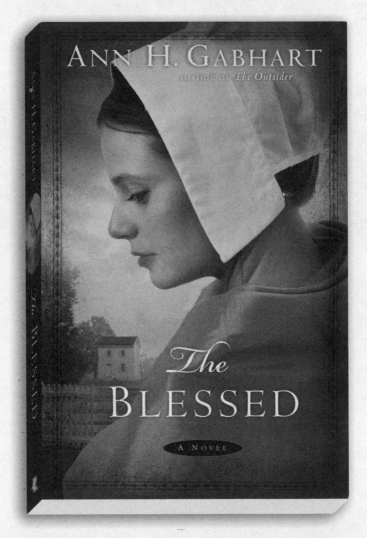

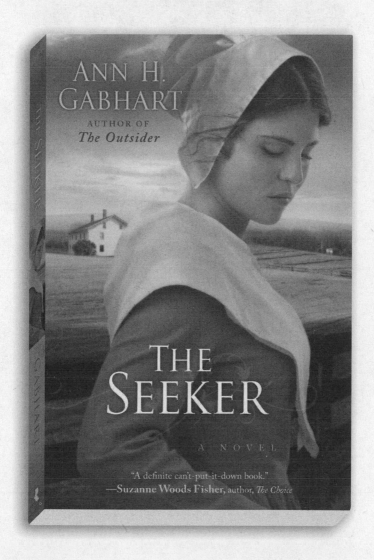